American Storytellers

Philip Baruth
American Zombie Beauty

Darrin Doyle
The Big Baby Crime Spree and Other Delusions

Joyce Hinnefeld
The Beauty of Their Youth

Rita Ciresi
Wild Boys

Dancing in Their Dead Mother's Dresses

Dancing in Their Dead Mother's Dresses

Stories

Doug Ramspeck

Wolfson Press

Grateful acknowledgment is made to the editors of the following publications where stories in this collection were originally published, sometimes in slightly different forms:

Bath Flash Fiction Awards: "Snow Crow"

Chautauqua Literary Journal: "Old Snow"

Cincinnati Review: "Rune"

The Georgia Review: "Winter Sky"

Hunger Mountain: "Occultations"

Lake Effect: "Dancing in Their Dead Mother's Dresses"

Narrative Magazine: "Through the Wall"

New Letters: "Migration"

The South Carolina Review: "Balloon" and "Omens"

The Southern Review: "A Map of Years"

Vestal Review: "Feral Prophecy"

"Snow Crow" received First Place in the Bath Flash Fiction 19th Award. "Balloon" was listed as a Distinguished Story for 2018 in *The Best American Short Stories*. "Old Snow" and "Feral Prophecy" were nominated for Pushcart Prizes.

Front cover by Kelcey Ervick
Interior design by Mali Bonnell and Julia Moreno

ISBN: 978-1-950066-28-5

Wolfson Press
Master of Liberal Studies Program
Indiana University South Bend
1700 Mishawaka Avenue
South Bend, Indiana 46634-7111

WolfsonPress.com

Contents

Foreword

"THIS IS THE UNIVERSE OF EVERYTHING," SAYS THE NARRATOR of "Balloons," the first story in this lyrical and luminous collection. The protagonist is nine-year-old Sophia, who also answers to "*Come here*" and "*Quiet*," and whose mother has died, leaving her with a distant father and a dog named Ketchup. Sophia is grieving, growing up, and listening to the secrets of the whispering creek. Her world is small, but her imagination is vast: together they form her universe of everything.

Doug Ramspeck's story collection, *Dancing in Their Dead Mother's Dresses*, is its own universe of everything. The stories feel set as much in the characters' imaginations as they are set in the Midwest. But the external surroundings of muddy Midwestern rivers, train bridges, and winter lakes are not just backdrops; they are sources of metaphors that help the characters make meaning of their often unsettling realities: dead mothers, absent fathers, sick siblings, inscrutable friends, intriguing neighbors, and unhappy wives. In this universe, the only way to process literal reality is through the language of metaphor. For example, in "A Map of Years," Cal thinks the ever-accruing years of his life are "like the ghost seeds of cottonwoods [that] slip away in the wind." Or maybe a year "is a doorway in the mind" or "a raft he rides," or, he thinks, "maybe years gather like stones at the bottom of the river." If he can find the right metaphor, the story seems to say, he might survive the ache in his hands from his job, his brother's impending death, or his years-long obsession with that same brother's wife.

The alliterative title, *Dancing in Their Dead Mother's Dresses*, hints at the lyrical language to come. It's easy to get carried away by the sentences of these stories, their sounds and sibilance, and in the characters whose inner worlds are as fully explored as the outer world. The collection is, unsurprisingly, written by a poet. Doug Ramspeck is the author of ten collections of poetry, one previous collection of short stories, and a novella. "Balloon" received a Distinguished Story citation in *The Best American Short Stories*. This is a collection by a writer, arguably at the pinnacle of his career as well as a master of his craft, who still writes with the urgency of someone with so many stories yet to tell, so many experiences to explore through language.

The narrative momentum of the stories is created not so much by a series of dramatic events as by an internal reckoning with a particular and often traumatic event that the characters are powerless to change. As they attempt to survive an event's aftermath, Ramspeck's characters are always searching for external signs—in nature, in dreams, and in their bodies. They listen to the creek's secret messages ("Balloon"), "to the language of [. . .] leaves" ("Rune"), or to a dead crow "calling [. . .] in the night, calling [. . .] in his dreams," ("Snow Crow"). In "Migrations," footprints become "hieroglyphics in the snow," and, in the title story, as the sisters dance in their dead mother's dresses, their arms are "waving an imaginary language. Some choreography of signs." It is a universe of animal carcasses, falling snow, and vast lakes, all of which get transformed through the power of language and metaphor into worlds of hope and longing and survival.

The characters are haunted, both by dead loved ones and by the silence they need to survive. In "Omens," after her brother dies, Abby demands that her best friend Evie never speak of him again. Evie agrees but she knows that she will "carry the silence always in her chest or her throat, carry it in Abby's presence, carry it like weeds that keep growing in a field till they take over." She knows that the silence will haunt them and their friendship: "She wanted to explain that to Abby, [. . .] that it would always be waiting there between them, always lurking, always watching them and passing judgment." Perhaps even more than the brother's death, it may be this silence that destroys their friendship.

In the two stories set in a large city—Chicago—the protagonists struggle to navigate the realities of their marriages. Lewis in "Through the Wall" finds marriage to be a "strange existence" and imagines encounters with the attractive neighbor whose apartment shares a wall with his. In "Winter Sky," Jason Abrams—who shot birds with a pellet gun when he was twelve—becomes, as an adult, the victim of random gun violence. The injury is just one of the ways his world has changed from the one he grew up in, where he'd fantasized about fighting Nazis and outlaws. As he convalesces, he reflects on how strange it is—"infuriating really"—to find himself the "patriarchal oppressor" in his own marriage.

Dancing in Their Dead Mother's Dresses calls to mind other language-rich contemporary story collections about the harsh realities of both the urban and rural Midwest: *The Luck of the Fall* and *Eight Mile High* by fellow poet Jim Ray Daniels; *Knockemstiff* by Donald Ray Pollock; and *American Salvage* by Bonnie Jo Campbell. But there are differences in setting, tone, style. Daniels's collections feature working-class, Detroit-based stories told primarily by first-person narrators who clearly want to tell you a tale. Ramspeck's stories are narrated in the closest third person possible, transporting readers to characters' inner worlds through free indirect discourse. Pollock's linked collection is set in the actual town of Knockemstiff, Ohio, where he was a resident, and the title sets the satirical tone that permeates the collection. Ramspeck's work might be most like that of Bonnie Jo Campbell, who writes with a starker realism, but who shares an interest in exploring the effects of traumatic events that destabilize the natural, man-made, and inner worlds.

All of these collections share a common ancestor in Sherwood Anderson's 1919 linked story collection *Winesburg Ohio*, but *Dancing in Their Dead Mother's Dresses* may be the closest stylistic relative, with its psychological explorations and poetic realism. In Anderson's story "Hands," the narrator proclaims: "The story of Wing Biddlebaum is a story of hands. Their restless activity, like unto the beating of the wings of an imprisoned bird, had given him his name. Some obscure poet of the town had thought of it." The hands of Anderson's story have a secret past—accusations of sexual abuse—that led Wing Biddlebaum to Winesburg. Doug Ramspeck takes a similarly poetic approach to his characters, with nuanced portraits and dark histories. The narrative kinship feels closest in Ramspeck's final story, the title story, which juxtaposes death and dancing, and where the narrator addresses the reader directly: "Listen," the story begins. "The thump of the music is threadbare on this

Sunday afternoon." And at the end, once again: "Listen: the thump of the music is threadbare." The girls are dancing, yes, in the dresses of their dead mother. Their mother is dead, but they must live on, and so they dance, "lift[ing] the folds of the dresses […] as though they"—the dresses—"might suddenly come alive."

In our circumscribed realities, where mothers die but children live on, or brothers die and siblings must live on, sometimes all we have are the worlds of our imaginations. At the end of "Old Snow" it is summertime, but Olivia holds a snow globe in her hand, and it becomes a metaphor for her own world, her universe of everything. She shakes it: "It is snowing in the world inside her hand. The world there is snowing."

Kelcey Ervick
Mishawaka, Indiana

For Beth and Lee

I.

Balloon

HER NAME IS SOPHIA AND ALSO *COME HERE* AND *QUIET* AND *Bring me one*. It is the time of summer when there is heat lightning in the distance but no rain, a little flash that barely makes a sound but seems to watch from the far horizon, beyond the soybean fields. Often, first thing out of bed, Sophia stands at her window and gazes at the flatness of the land and at the gray light and at the stillness of the road. The road usually says *Nothing* or *I am a held breath*. Later it will collect the day's heat and hold it so it hurts her feet if she walks on it. Dust will rise from its body. Sophia is nine. She counts the number on her fingers. When late August at last arrives, the bus will stop in front of her house again and wait with its yellow eye. She will climb aboard and feel the gravity of everyone turning in her direction. Their attention will lock on, saying, *You don't have a mother anymore* or *Don't sit by me*.

Ketchup lies at Sophia's feet, her chin on her paws. She is part German shepherd, part retriever. She watches Sophia at the window. She has a pink tongue that droops out of the side of her mouth in summer weather. She is all black except for a few white markings on her paws and chest. Ketchup sleeps each night in Sophia's bed and puts her ears up on those rare occasions when a car or truck whooshes past on the road. The dog was found by Sophia's mother, half-starved by the creek behind the house, gnawing on a plastic ketchup bottle. Apparently you could see her ribs. Her fur was matted and dirty. Now Sophia brushes Ketchup's fur each day with the same brush she uses on her own hair. This is the universe of everything.

Now, bracing herself, Sophia climbs down the stairs to the kitchen. Her father looks up from where he is sitting with a bowl of cereal. He is shirtless. His skin is dark on his shoulders and neck and arms, but his chest is pale as a grub. He affixes her with his eyes and points at Ketchup. He says, "Don't forget about tonight. No reminders. I'm not playing around."

"Okay," Sophia says.

The creek today is a living thing. Sophia walks along its edge, Ketchup running beside her. Her father has left for work. The creek hides down its narrow trench, past a curtain of tall grass. The water winds this way and that. These days it is barely a trickle, a little gurgle. Sometimes, in certain moods, Sophia imagines that it is whispering a secret message that only she can understand. And what does it say? It announces that there are eyes behind the clouds or that the clouds are ears pointing at the land, listening. Or maybe it is Sophia's mother who is listening from so high up.

Sophia sits in the grass and studies the water as it slips by. She rubs Ketchup behind her ears. One of her earliest memories is of a leaf floating in the muddy waters. It was a raft. Sophia imagines that it was off on a journey, an adventure. But to where? What dreams might a leaf have? Her mother is there in the memory as well. She is saying they should race leaves, and so they do. And what sound does a leaf make in the water as it slips past? It says *Silence* or *Soon I'll be out of sight* or *Goodbye*. Why Sophia remembers this day with the leaves she cannot say. A leaf is a kind of love, she thinks, something that belongs just to you. "Look at that," her mother is saying in the memory. "Look at how fast they are going."

Sophia feels the day stretching outward. It doesn't want to end. She sits cross-legged on the grass in the backyard, throwing a green tennis ball for Ketchup. The dog races after the ball and chomps it in her mouth. It is wet when she hands it back. Sophia throws it again, and there is something about the arc that seems like a kind of vision or prayer. First it goes up, alive and free, and then it comes back down. And Sophia, as she watches the dog running, feels herself becoming almost invisible. She is slipping away from the world. Maybe Ketchup will turn around with the ball in her mouth and be stunned. No one will be sitting there. Sophia thinks this while a bee is hovering above the clover beside her knee. The little white flower is a kind of forever. It lives in the grass that lives in the yard. It disappears each year but then comes back. It is somehow more real than anything.

Later she turns on the sprinkler and watches it turning one way then the next. This is how the day goes. She runs through the sprinkler, and Ketchup, at a safe distance, barks.

It was a little pop in the brain. Sophia is remembering this while lying in her bed. The sheet over her face. She is statuary. The game is hide-and-seek. She told Ketchup to *Stay* in the hallway, then she herself came into the room to hide. Then she called out. Now she hears Ketchup sniffing at the side of the bed. But what Sophia is imagining is a balloon you blow too hard. It swells and swells then suddenly there's a loud noise. She tries to picture it, but at once Ketchup is jumping on the bed. Sophia removes the sheet and throws her arms around the dog's neck. "Here I am," she says. But she is still thinking about that balloon popping in her mother's head while she was at work.

Later she goes down the stairs to make ham sandwiches. There is one for her and one for Ketchup. They eat on the back stoop. Her thoughts grow jumbled as she is chewing. She has always liked the deadheads of dandelions. How they are carried off in a wind. How they are old in their white hair. And if you blow on the flowers, they come apart. She thinks: *My mother's brain was a white flower. Someone blew on it.* Then her mother was hidden beneath a mound of dirt. Sophia pictures herself standing there beside her father at the cemetery. Her father is gripping her hand too hard. It hurts.

There are names for days that keep going and going: *The sun is too hot* or *Running my fingers through my mother's dresses* or *Filling Ketchup's water bowl* or *Here are my dolls* or *Watching cartoons*. Sophia's name as the day persists is *I'm not really here* or *My mother is the sound of the birds in the trees* or *The tall grass is talking* or *My father will be mad if I don't chain her*.

Sophia is standing in the backyard. She's looking at how the long leash is attached to a metal stake in the ground. There is a hook she is supposed to connect to Ketchup's collar. She tries it then steps away. Ketchup strains at the length of it, desperate to follow. Ketchup barks. And the bark says, *Let me come with you*. Sophia lets the dog free and they walk together up to the front of the house and the road. She squints in both directions, and what does she see? Straightness. Emptiness. Glaring sunlight. The soybean field across the road seems to rustle like water in the wind. It is muttering a small sound.

A half hour later, Sophia pulls a plastic box from under the bed that once belonged to both her parents. It is her father's bed now. She removes a bright red ribbon and a bow for wrapping gifts. She affixes the bow to Ketchup's head with the ribbon. Ketchup holds still at first, but then she tilts her head downward and tries to remove it with a paw.

"You look beautiful," Sophia says.

Soon she is naming the afternoon *Flipping through the pages of a book* and *Seeing how long I can hold my breath* and *Watching Ketchup watch a squirrel on a limb out the window.*

Her father is home. He says, "Bring me a beer. Leave it outside the bathroom door." Later, when he's out of the shower, he says, "Is it done . . . she's out on her chain?" Later, when his wet hair is slicked back, he says, "Put something nicer on." After that he says, "I'm picking up the pizza. If she shows up before I get back, let her in. Got it?" Finally, when he's holding the keys to his truck, he says, "You be nice to her . . . hear me? You don't want to find out what happens otherwise."

Sophia nods. Her head has learned to bob at the appropriate moments. Her father doesn't look at her while he talks. He speaks to the air or his hands or the world outside the windows. Once he told her, "I didn't sign up for being a parent by myself. That's not how it works."

Then he is gone from the house. Sophia stands at the picture window at the back of the living room. The lawn grass is browning with summer. The trees at the yard's edge are motionless. The clouds are pale white scars above them. The creek is invisible. And Ketchup is pacing, testing and testing the length of the tether, which yanks her suddenly if she ventures too far. She is trying to get back into the house, trying to get back to Sophia. Finally she lies down and remains there like a ghost.

Sophia slips out the back door and hugs her.

The woman's name is Betsy and *Her father's new girlfriend* and *Allergic to dogs* and *Not my mother*. She is sitting at the dining room table. She looks like Mrs. Greene, who Sophia had in kindergarten. It's the red hair and freckles. It's the way she leans too close to you when she talks.

"Your father says you do very well in school," she says.

"I guess," Sophia says.

"You must be very smart," the woman says.

Sophia shrugs.

"Is school your favorite?" the woman asks.

"No," Sophia says.

"Oh. You don't like school?"

"No," Sophia says.

"It's boring? I know I felt that way."

"No, I like learning."

"Then what?" the woman asks.

"Everyone looks at you."

"That's bad?" the woman asks.

Ketchup is barking from outside as they talk. The sound burrows deep down into Sophia's ear. The sound says, *Please,*

please. Sophia, meanwhile, is studying the flowers on the woman's dress. They are little pink flowers. They are so small she almost has to squint to see them, and even then they hardly exist.

"Is that barking bothering you?" her father suddenly asks the woman. The sound of his voice is a shudder. It moves up and down Sophia's ribs. It tickles over her skin. She looks up, stiffening in place.

"It's fine," the woman says.

"You don't like dogs?" Sophia blurts.

The woman has just taken a bite of pizza. She chews. She dabs a napkin across her mouth. She says, "It's not that, Honey. They make me sneeze and my eyes water. It's always been like that. I like them from afar."

There is a gap in her two front teeth as she smiles. Sophia can see the pink little creature of her tongue.

"I explained this already," her father says.

"What if she doesn't get close?" Sophia says.

"I'm sorry, Sweetie."

"Be polite," her father warns.

"Oh, she's fine," the woman says. "Just look at her. She's darling. You didn't tell me your daughter was so delightful."

"Can't you shut her up?" her father asks.

"What's her name?" the woman asks.

Sophia says, "Ketchup."

"Really?" the woman asks.

"Shut that dog up," her father says. "Move her farther from the house."

"My mother found her eating ketchup," Sophia says.

"That's about enough," her father says.

"I'm so sorry about your mother," the woman says.

Sophia says *Nothing*. She says *Silence*.

The woman says, "Your Dad told me it's been fourteen months now. Is that right? How hard it must be for both of you. You're so brave."

"Do you want another beer?" her father asks.

"I don't mind if I do," the woman says.

Sophia's father gives Sophia the look. Up she jumps. She sees Ketchup out the window. She is facing the house. She seems to twitch a little with each bark.

"I hope to be over here a lot more now," the woman says when Sophia hands her the bottle. "But don't think I'm trying to be a replacement, Honey. I know better."

"My name is Sophia," Sophia says.

"Don't get mouthy," her father says.

"She's fine," the woman says.

"How often?" Sophia asks.

"Oh, I don't know."

"What about Ketchup?" Sophia asks.

Her father's hand reaches out from his chair, grabs her arm high on the wrist, squeezes hard. Too hard. His eyes are like falling off a cliff.

"Go out there and shut your dog up," he says. "Do you hear me? Or do you want me to drop her off at the pound tomorrow? Do you understand what I'm saying?"

"Oh, it's fine, Honey, really," the woman is saying.

And Sophia is thinking: *His name isn't Honey either*. And *She's the devil.*

She walks Ketchup by the creek. The water looks lonesome in its thin line. It barely has the strength to go on. She has a theory that mosquitoes can't find you if you hold your breath and stand so still you aren't actually there. She closes her eyes at one point and aims her face toward the sun, which is dipping down behind the trees. When she opens her eyes, Ketchup is looking at her. Each time she glances at her dog, the tail begins to wag. She thinks of what it's like in school when you move down the hallways. She keeps her eyes on her shoes and hugs close to the walls. And she thinks of walking out beyond the creek, into the trees, walking until she reaches the cemetery where her mother is resting beneath the dirt. But she doesn't actually know which way she would have to walk to get there. She imagines her mother lying in the ground and dreaming of the moon and the stars she can't see. She must dream that the moon is a moth, and the stars are white bees. She must dream of her daughter and of Ketchup, and maybe she whispers beneath the ground. And what does she say? *There you are. I see you. There you both are. I see you. I see you.*

Her father is a frown. His whole face swivels into it. He leans over the bed and pulls the sheet up to her chin.

He says, "You have to be nicer to her."

His breath is beer. He says, "People matter more than dogs. Do you understand me?"

He says, "You need a woman in your life. There are things I don't know."

He says, "Don't embarrass me again."

He says, "This doesn't mean I'm forgetting your mother."

He says, "Go to sleep."

He says, "That damn dog better not start barking again."

He says, "Dogs belong outside anyway. I've given you too much slack. Because you know why."

He says, "No more sleeping in your bed."

He says, "Behave now."

And so she clamps shut her eyes when he is gone. This is what sleep is. You clamp shut your eyes and wait for it to come. She thinks of it, sometimes, as like a balloon deflating. The air goes out of it and then you sleep. But she keeps hearing, now, voices in the wall. They slosh like suds. It is her father and her in the next room. Her name is *High scratchy voice* and *Frilly giggle*. Sophia knows they are in her mother's bedroom. They are talking. They are soap suds. Sophia imagines that she can slip inside those soap suds and fall asleep, but it doesn't happen. Then—later—the voices are finally gone from the bedroom. She hears them, instead, from the living room. The television is on. She reaches for Ketchup in the bed, but Ketchup isn't there. She hugs her pillow to her chest and pretends it is Ketchup. And the fury she feels in her body is a blossom. It is a sudden flower. It is perfect in its shape.

And she imagines that Ketchup's name is *I am lonely in the yard* and *It's so dark out here* and *I miss Sophia* and *What did I do to deserve this?*

Barking. Sophia sits up in bed. Night falls through her window. Night dresses the sky beyond her curtains. Barking. Her bare feet are on the floorboards. Barking. The sounds of insects fill the space between the barks. She sneaks out from her bedroom and climbs down the stairs. She cups her hands around her eyes to look out. Barking. But she can't see Ketchup anywhere. Barking. Soon, Sophia knows, her father's voice will be a trumpet. It will sound in the house. So she rushes back to her bedroom and drags her comforter from the bed. She drags it behind her down the stairs. She drags it out the kitchen door and into the backyard. Barking. She feels the prickles of the grass against her feet. She feels the coolness of the air. The black of her dog is invisible in the black of the night. The dog isn't really there. She's a ghost. Barking. Then Ketchup is rushing up against her, pressing against her. Ketchup wriggles and licks and can't hold still. This is everything. This is more than the stars hiding behind the clouds, more than the moon impaled in the trees. Sophia spreads the comforter and lies down. For a time—a long time—Ketchup is too excited to lie down, but finally she does. Ketchup releases a big sigh. She rolls on her back to have her belly rubbed. If it were light out, Sophia knows, she could see the pink of that belly. But now there is just the thump of the tail, even while she's on her back. And Sophia closes her eyes and names the day behind them *Just a bad day*, something her mother liked to say. A day, her mother made it sound, that would soon give way, as easy as snapping fingers. But Sophia knows a secret: some days pop like a balloon and ruin everything.

A Map Of Years

THE FIRST WARNING HE HEARS WHISPERING IS A HAWK. IT MUST have levitated out of the cut of the muddy river, up into the living air. Then the route must have carried it past the yellowing soybean fields and the corn as still as statuary, across the drainage verge and the county road, and into the small Ohio neighborhood of lawns and arcing sprinklers and overturned bicycles. It is here where Cal, thirty-one, is sipping beer in a backyard and gazing toward the crowd. He is out of focus in his thoughts, ill-at-ease in his own body. He is mostly watching his brother, Marvin, who is thirty-four, watching Marvin's wife, Patty, who is thirty-two, watching the older girl, Joyce, who is nine, and watching the youngest, little Donny, whose seventh birthday is exactly today. Cal stands at a distance, and this is when the hawk's shadow slips above the chain link fence to make its passage across the lawn. It angles above the trampoline and the outdoor grill near the birthday boy's grandparents, angles toward Patty. She is dressed today in a two-piece blue bathing suit, a floppy white T-shirt extending over her deeply tanned thighs. She is perched in a green plastic lawn chair with crossed legs, is twirling the raised foot in a mesmerizing orbit. She is sipping pink lemonade through a bent straw. The shadow, next, passes the clothesline and a Frisbee and two nearly deflated balloons that have skittered within a few feet of the house. Cal, looking up, tries to find the geography of wings, but the sun is a smear, a blur, a subtracting indeterminacy. And then the shadow, without hesitation, passes directly into the body of his brother. It bisects the chest, vanishing. Cal's brother, in that instant, shudders as though from a blow, shudders into a seizure of his shoulders and arms. Then a fist comes up and he is coughing, coughing, coughing. It seems he is trying to expel something untoward, something dark and unexpected, something that has apparently lodged itself deep within him. Cal starts heading toward his brother—surely something unfathomable is occurring—but then, a moment later, Marvin is laughing again and sipping his beer again and demonstrating, to a friend beside him, his putting form.

Then it is winter. There are moments, at work, when the pain in Cal's hands becomes for him almost dreamlike, when he envisions the ache of it hiding in the deepest and most hidden tissue of his knuckles and fingers. And it is like watching smoke rise along the hills from a distant and ghostly fire. The factory where he works—twenty miles from Conway—manufactures mostly living room furniture. All day he pulls the upholstery stitching tighter and tighter, dragging it upward over the frames. And he thinks as he works, memories flitting back, like the time his brother told him snow was bits of the moon that had broken loose, that it began as white ash but froze drifting to the land. Cal worried as a boy that eventually the night moon would simply come apart and vanish. He imagines this while his peers at the plant lift their voices toward the corrugated ceiling, while he is driving home on County Route 9, while he is sitting alone at his kitchen table or watching the dull sea of the television. Late most nights he falls into bed and the real bout of pain begins. It burrows in like an ice pick.

Often he rises at least once to fill the kitchen sink with cold water and ice cubes. Then he thrusts in his hands and waits for the perfect reverie of numbness. He allows his thoughts to drift to faint images and recollections of his brother, who is a manager at Dorigan's—the furniture plant—and who got him his job and has always been his one true protector in the world. Marvin actually graduated from Bowling Green State University, the only member of the family to ever do such a thing. He has the black gown he wore for the occasion, the mortarboard hat with a tassel that bobbed when he walked. And Marvin often invites Cal to his home for meals and to watch football and the loud crashing of bodies.

And Cal allows himself certain thoughts about Patty as well—though other thoughts he banishes. Her middle name is Camille, which seems to him as exotic as a foreign land. Once, all of them went tubing in the river from where the hawk rose. They waded into the muddy and insistent current, felt the tug of its passage like a gravity. They floated beneath the canopy of leaves, light flickering its undulating messages. Later Patty cut her foot on a rock. Marvin and the kids had floated far ahead, so it was left to Cal to dab at the welling blood with Kleenexes. He held the ankle like an offering in his hands, placed two Band-Aids across the jagged fissure of the wound.

"Go on without me," Patty said. "I'll sit here until all of you come back."

"I'll stay," Cal said.

"No, no. Don't miss the fun."

"I'll stay."

Cal enjoys the indulgence of memory in the bitter of winter

when his hands are in the sink after midnight, when sleep eludes him. There is nothing wrong with this particular memory, he tells himself. Nothing out of place. It fits with the world the way it should. So he closes his eyes and lets the power of the ice insinuate itself into his hands, to freeze the pain into a solid block that is easier to bear. And he admits to himself—softly, softly—that the memory of holding Patty's foot is probably the happiest of his life. The years, then, are a raft he rides. One moment it is dead summer and the air is a weight pressing in, and the next bright leaves make a fluttering of confetti in the air. Or maybe ice shimmers in the bar ditches along the roadside as he drives home. The passage of days is often in his thoughts on McDamler Road when he heads past the refinery flames along the outskirts of town, seeing men in striped pants along the grassy median, spearing trash. Then he drives past the prison itself and studies the razor wire. He imagines life inside the walls as comprised of rising in the morning and letting the hours seep their way into the body. He wonders if it is possible for decades to seem like the sun speared by the trees at dusk, like when he walks to his car and his breaths are a vapor in the winter chill, lifting like a prayer.

And often he thinks about his brother, worries. He remembers the shadow of the hawk impaling Marvin's chest. And it's not just that. Every few weeks his brother takes him to the shopping mall on the edges of Conway. They go bowling or maybe for ribs or to drink beer, and they talk in familiar voices about work or their parents or Marvin's kids or the Buckeyes or tax season or the annoyance of long trains at railroad crossings or the deer that always seem to be leaping across the rural roads. And once, on the drive there, Cal notices bits of leaf meal clinging to his brother's hair. It is just above the right ear, holding close, and it seems so out of place that Cal knows it must be a sign. And as they walk together through the main doors of Buffalo Wild Wings, he notices, too, a strange and almost fetid scent emanating from his brother. It is like the green film that forms sometimes on the surface of a stagnant pond. And then, in late February, in an ice storm, a thick tree branch from a hickory drops of its own volition out of the sky. It caves in the roof of the toolshed where Marvin keeps his riding mower. And then there appears—it must be April or May—a discoloration of skin along Marvin's temple. It is a patch that seems in the shape of a map of an ancient world, older than the moon. But by summer it disappears except for a pale geography of a shadow. And then, in July, they are walking one evening in Devlon Park when Marvin is stung on the neck by a black wasp with an elongated body. And not even a week after that, Cal and Marvin are walking again—this time near the woods by the reservoir—when a skinny snake maybe two feet long wiggles through the tall grass. It passes like an oracle along the dirt path then directly over Marvin's work boot before muscling away into the undergrowth.

"What the hell?" Marvin says.

The summer sun is an orange orb slipping low to the land at day's end. It is a messenger of tinged light on the cusp of the woods. Cal, watching, thinks to himself that love is forever what they are trying to wrestle away from you.

His earliest memories of his brother are sounds. They are something he has ferried with him since childhood. He imagines Marvin's voice forming the shape of the word. *Goof. Goof.* Marvin still speaks the nickname affectionately from time to time, making a playful tune of it. *Hey, Goof, sew your head on straight. Slow down, Goof, and let your thoughts catch up.* Always he is smiling as he says this, squeezing a hand to his brother's shoulder. There is something comforting in the name. And with it are so many fragments of memories, a collage like the great trends and movements and advancements and descents he studied in history at school. He pictures, from childhood, his brother's red and white bobber in the river. He sees his own bobber beside it. And he envisions wrestling with Marvin in the backyard or riding in the back seat of the van on their way to Michigan and the home of their grandparents. And he recalls himself and his brother sitting side by side on the yellow bus on the way to school, and he visualizes Marvin taking a wild swing at an orange-haired boy who once bloodied Cal's nose beneath the viaduct on Wallace Avenue. And there is the sound of playing cards being shuffled and Marvin's girlfriends in high school and Patty brought home from college for the first time. In Cal's memory she squints then shakes his hand with a strange formality. And there is the church where Cal—in what may be his proudest moment—is Marvin's best man. And later there are the wrinkled faces and the cries and the rancid diapers of the babies. And there is the job at the plant and the cycles of the moon and Marvin insisting on every birthday, every holiday, every every, that Cal be there, that Cal is family, that Cal is loved. This is, of course, a kind of mystery on the order of the ants that appeared one summer in great profusion in Cal's shower stall, pooled by the drain, then vanished as quickly as they'd arrived.

The autumn he turns forty, Cal has surgery on his left hand. There is a moment while he is drifting into the anesthesia that he feels lighter than the world itself. This is in the cold basement of

St. Mary's. And he thinks, for some reason, of prayers. As a boy he imagined them rising toward the church rafters and beyond. They slipped, it seemed, easily into air, rising past the trees and then the clouds, out from the planet itself. They journeyed into the stars and beyond, lonely in their passage. Then they arrived at that great and waiting Ear, the First Ear, the Listening Ear. And when Cal wakes, when he is being driven by his brother away from the hospital, when the sky outside the windshield is brooding low to the earth, he becomes acquainted with a new kind of pain. There are great waves of it in his hand, searing and hot, like something being shorn away. He stays at his brother's house for the recovery—Marvin and Patty insist. He lives in the finished basement, in the small low-ceilinged space between the family den and the laundry room. He has his own private bathroom, his own single bed. Those first nights he barely sleeps at all, despite the pain medication. He lies awake and imagines that his hand has swollen to twice its normal size, that it is a clod hand, a beast hand, like something you would see tied up with butcher's string. And he listens to the low animal sighs of the furnace, to the living mechanical gurgle of the sump pump. He hears footsteps muffled on the ceiling and the occasional and hallucinatory flushing of a toilet from the first floor.

Soon there is the crowdedness to the days. At first he has difficulty adjusting. It's as though he has migrated from empty countryside into a great city center, where the commotion of activity and voices is deafening. And it starts early, in the gray indistinctness of morning. There are voices and music and slamming doors reverberating through the house, then the family gathering at the breakfast table. Donny is fifteen now, Joyce seventeen, both in high school, both always running late. They pour quick bowls of cereal and drink Mountain Dew. And

Marvin has a smoothie and Patty has a large mug of coffee and sometimes a blueberry bagel smeared with low-fat cream cheese. And, throughout, there is the buzzing hive of voices, sometimes rancorous, sometimes teasing, sometimes sleepy and sullen. They arrive rapidly, jumbling one atop the next, often indecipherable. Then the cars vanish from the drive as everyone leaves for school or for work, and Cal is exiled with the border collie, Morrie, who lies in a rectangle of sunlight on the living room floor. Cal exists then in a quietude that leaves an open space for the ache and the throb of his fingers.

His favorite time of day is when Patty returns. She works half days as a receptionist at a dentist's office in Conway. But by the time the sun is just beginning its descent toward the river, when he sees out the back windows the light filtering down through the trees and making a glimmering atop the gray current, she comes through the front door and puts down her purse. At once her words are a gift, tumbling out without a care or a concern. He is in a thrall. He thinks of the persistence of a waterfall, splashing. And he studies the fine character lines in her face, how there is a growing perfection to her as the years accumulate. And he notices, too, the crooked left incisor that crosses the tooth beside it, and the first gray hairs. And he knows that he is happy in this life.

One day she takes him to shop for new clothes, to "spruce him up." Another they drive to his apartment so she can suggest a few updates, a coat of paint, some new furniture, maybe a print or two for the walls. But most days they simply sit in the back yard and sip Diet Cokes. It is as though there is nothing else in the world except the slack sun above them, the itinerant clouds, and the discursive way her voice flits like a perfect and bright bird. Then one afternoon she defends him fiercely at Walmart. They are in the checkout lane when a clerk asks about what happened to his hand. He starts to explain, but, after he attempts a few words, the clerk turns instead to Patty, asks her. A moment later the clerk turns back to Cal, speaks in a loud and slow voice, enunciating carefully. And in the parking lot a few minutes later, surrounded by the glare and shimmer of a wild herd of cars, Patty is clearly furious. She insists that the woman was being inconsiderate, offensive. She tells Cal that he has always been far, far brighter than people give him credit for. She says it's mainly just his social skills, that he shouldn't take it personally. In truth, though, Cal doesn't actually feel insulted. He liked the way the woman twirled her slender silver necklace as she spoke, reminding him, for some reason, of a woman in a fairy tale conjuring hidden spirits. But he nods as Patty speaks, feels the welcome pressure of her hand against his shoulder, the thumb curling faintly around his right collarbone. It is as though she is holding him there in place, fixing him forever in this one position. She is preventing the rotation of the planet from sending him slipping and tumbling off the face of it into the stratosphere.

A life, it seems, exists as though in that in-between time of waking and sleeping, whispering like that hawk from so long ago. And there is a way in which Cal often feels—whether he is working at the furniture plant or sitting on his couch or eating tacos at his brother's house or driving in heavy snow—that he is waiting for something. He has been sensing it gathering for so long, a great train in the distance with the howl of its horn, splitting darkness, cracking it open like a shell. And then when he is forty-nine, his brother fifty-two, it actually arrives.

The symptoms, at first, are as small as those pretend teacups girls play with as children. Everyone remarks that Marvin has lost a little weight. Then, in short order, he complains of back pain and a general feeling of listlessness. For a long time there is no diagnosis, but by July there is the bloating and severe abdominal pain and the darkened urine. It is Patty who tells Cal this. And then there is the loss of appetite and the jaundice. Soon the doctors are certain, are telling Marvin they should operate right away. The way Cal hears all of this reminds him of when he gets water in his ear while swimming and the world outside of him feels very far away. It's not something he knows much about, after all. Pancreatic cancer.

Everything happens quickly after that, so quickly it is not easy even to breathe. After the surgery, there is the long incision in Marvin's belly. He appears old now, lying in bed at home or at the hospital, his eyes sunk back into his skull, as though attempting to disappear. His skin is sallow and sweating. Soon there is radiation and chemotherapy, and then Marvin is forever sick to his stomach, has to force himself to eat, can barely stand. Cal sits at his bedside at Marvin's home, and the kids are back periodically from their distant lives, and Patty is always collapsing into tears. Her face comes apart with it, and Cal can't help but imagine those hawk talons, that beak, that dark flapping of wings. By October Marvin is in hospice care, and the building's chairs are uncomfortable, and there's a smell Cal can't quite place but that reminds him of when, as a child, mice died in the walls of the basement. Much of the time, Marvin doesn't know where he is or who is sitting there beside him. Once he thinks Cal is their old boss from the furniture factory. Another time Patty is leaning by the bed and gripping her husband's hand in both of her own, but Marvin doesn't seem to realize she is there. He is drifting somewhere else, his thoughts like charred ash floating out above the land, glowing orange but aimless. Cal remembers to cry when Patty cries, when Joyce cries, when Donny cries. But the rest of the time it is like he has placed his entire body in the ice, has dipped his head beneath the surface.

Then Patty is telling him over the phone one morning that Marvin is gone. The suffering is over. He died in the night, his last breath releasing itself into the universe. Cal is at work when he hears this, standing in the break room where he has just taken a bite of a coconut cream donut. The sugar is sticky and unwelcome against his tongue. Then a tie clinches at his throat at the funeral service at the Trinity United Methodist Church. The pews there are the same unresisting surface against his legs he remembers from childhood. Then, at the cemetery, there is an open mouth of dirt, and Marvin is placed inside it. The sun is directly above them, a plucked eye. Surely none of this is actually happening, Cal thinks. He knows he should say something to Patty and the kids, but his tongue is in a tourniquet. Then they are walking back to the cars and he sees a gray squirrel with a twitching tail high on a limb. Then he is driving away from the cemetery, but the road isn't really there either, or maybe it is. It occurs to him that this is the only life he knows, the life he is consigned to. He stops at the light and somewhere inside him his heart is thrashing on and on, is dumb substance, and there is nothing else.

They are, it seems, like the ghost seeds of cottonwoods. They are white and wispy. And they slip away in a wind or float off because they are so light in their bodies. Or maybe, Cal thinks, a year is simply a doorway in the sky or a doorway in the mind or a doorway in the side of the mountain . . . or a door flapping in a breeze. Or maybe years gather like stones at the bottom of a river, smoothed out and growing slippery in the current. But now that his brother has left him, the years, it often seems, are somehow holding their breaths, are those deep gulps before you fling yourself from a diving board, are those spaces between heartbeats. His right hand, now, is the familiar pain, an agony he welcomes. But most nights he soaks both hands in the sink, filling it with ice. And he nods to his coworkers when they tell him how sorry they are, what a great guy his brother was. And he visits Patty several times a week, brings her groceries or climbs up on a ladder to clear away the stench of gunk from her gutters. Sometimes he pushes the mower across the wild growth of grass, or he carries softening salt from the back of his trunk into her house. And he vows to be there with a shovel for every snow that winter, and he sits with her in the kitchen that is as quiet now as a cloud. She looks down at her hands and tells him that her life feels fragmented, all these little pieces that don't add up. And she tells him about the first time she saw Marvin—in a campus library, of all places—and how she thought he looked conceited, too sure of himself. She is grinning as she says it, but then she has to peer out the window toward the lawn and the fields and the river and the trees and the grayness of the late autumn light and the clouds carrying dusk in their underbellies.

Then one night in late January, a Saturday, she phones after midnight. Her voice is a distortion in his ear as he rouses himself from sleep. He drives the four miles to her house, and the door comes open before he rings the bell. He is not an expert in such things, but he can tell she has been drinking. It is white wine she craves these days. It seeps deep into her blood and comes out as a mangled imprecision of words. He thinks of the wasps he and his brother used to watch as boys, how they fed on the fallen and fermenting crab apples in the backyard. They tumbled over on their backs and hummed, or flew erratically in air. She is sitting beside him on the couch, touching his hands and his legs as she talks. It is as though it is possible to press a word directly to the skin, to tattoo it there. And suddenly she is crying. He knows this because she is there inside his arms, and her face is pressed against his neck. He feels the wetness. And he thinks to himself that Patty probably believes he knows nothing of these things, that he has probably never had a girlfriend or even a kiss. But this isn't true. He remembers his late twenties, thinks of the nakedness of a particular woman. She was a statue there before his eyes, with long black hair covering her shoulders and parts of her breasts. Her name was Janice. He can't say he knew her very long—she broke it off. But the memory reminds him of how the pain in his hand comes and goes, goes and comes. Love, maybe, runs along that same strange circuitry. But now—right now—is a moment he will always remember, that will follow him into old age. He knows he will return to it again and again. All at once Patty pulls her head free from his neck, and the world of her face is salt and wet, and her eyes are pink and bleared, and strands of hair are clinging to her cheek. He knows, in this instant, that he might press his lips forward, might push the prow of his mouth against hers. This might actually happen—after so many decades. But instead, of course, he helps her stand from the couch. He tells her she should go to bed, assists her to the bedroom. She is slurring sounds about what a good friend he is, her best friend remaining in the world. He closes the door to her bedroom and drives into the snow that is coming down in a sudden fury. His headlights are streaming out before him. The snow is alive in the light, but also ghostly. He wants to drive and drive and drive, his fingers aching on the wheel. He wants to carry himself through his life like this, his neck still damp and perfected from Patty's tears, the sky a great and distant veil.

Winter Sky

IT WAS UNCLEAR TO JASON ABRAMS, EVEN AFTER THE ENCOUNTER near the Clark Street Bridge, whether his fascination with violence as a boy tracked within the normal range. He'd grown up in the northern suburb of Winnetka, four blocks from the lake, and one of his earliest memories was of a Civil War book his father kept in the study, complete with depictions of famous battles—renderings of fallen soldiers and blood stains and missing limbs and smoke from cannon fire. His favorite childhood pastime was to imagine—either by himself or with friends—that he was fighting Nazis with a Tommy gun, or was a sheriff or an outlaw with a six-shooter, or a spy with a Beretta, or a Viking with a Carolingian sword. Then there was the pellet gun for his twelfth birthday, after which blue jays and sparrows and robins and grackles were felled with such frequency in the woods behind the house that Jason became accustomed to the sight of the wounded creatures twitching their way free of the body, to a sprawl of feathers dropping from summer limbs.

Later, at New Trier High School, he played football for three years, imagining that one test of a person's mettle was not only what punishment he could mete out as a linebacker but also what punishment he could sustain. By the time he atttended Amherst College, his tendencies were exercised only in the viewing of occasional films alive with gunfire and explosions. And by the time he completed law school at the University of Chicago, had passed the Illinois Bar Exam, had met and had married Marjorie, and had had his first job that would lead him—after many years of punishing sixty-hour work weeks—to a limited partnership at Briggs and Ellis, LLP, he assumed that such aggressive tendencies were applied only to the convoluted threats and actualities of corporate litigation. He and his wife were patrons of the Chicago Symphony, after all, great readers of biographies and memoirs, fans of Pinter and Chekhov and Mamet, and had two declawed and sleepy cats living with them in their expansive condominium in the Gold Coast neighborhood. He was sixty-three now, his wife two years older, and he was certain that his colleagues and friends would describe him as more cerebral than physical, a thoughtful and distinguished gentleman, civilized and even soft-spoken, impeccable in his manners, and without, as they say, a violent bone in his body.

So now that he was finally home after ten days in Northwestern Memorial Hospital, now that the worst of the tides of physical pain and surges of exhaustion had dwindled to something almost manageable, he found himself thinking again and again about what had transpired beside the bridge. He remembered the business luncheon with the two lawyers from CNA Financial, remembered leaving the steak house that overlooked the Chicago River, and walking quickly down the sidewalk. He recalled watching the snow dropping into the river and disappearing, swallowed into nothingness. And that was when he had looked up, briefcase in hand, to see a teenage boy approaching with a handgun stuck out before him, his arm locked, the dark weapon extended like a bayonet. The boy appeared skinny to the point of emaciation, with a navy-blue stocking cap and a flannel shirt, no coat, his breaths expelling before him in agitated mists. Suddenly the weapon was jabbed against Jason's ribs, poking. The boy asked for a wallet, a watch. His voice was hushed, almost whispered.

Now, as Jason lay in bed watching his wife dressing in a dark pantsuit for work, he envisioned once more the boy's oversized Adam's apple thrashing in his throat, his face flushed pink with cold, his eyes wild beneath where the stocking cap left off. It would have been a simple enough matter, of course, for Jason to reach into his back pocket and to hand over the couple of hundred dollars in cash, to relinquish his credit cards, to unclasp the Breguet from his wrist (even though it had been a gift from Marjorie for his sixtieth birthday), to file a police report and an insurance claim. Securing a new driver's license and membership card to the Winterfield Squash Club would have been a nuisance, but soon the event would have transformed into an entertaining story to tell his executive assistant and his colleagues, to share at cocktail parties and dinner events, to embellish for his grown son and daughter—both, as things had turned out, living in New Mexico—the next time they spoke by phone. The encounter, after all, was nothing but a mere blink of a moment in a life that had been—at least until recently—mostly generous with challenging and fulfilling experiences. So why had he hesitated? Why had he let that sudden rush of furious adrenaline persuade him to sweep out an arm in an attempt to knock the gun free?

The condominium Jason shared with his wife was on the seventeenth floor, so, propped up in the king-sized bed, he could see the winter grays of the sky and Lake Michigan, the two seeming to form on the horizon into one. Near the shore there were frozen patches of water, but farther out the gray was liquid, a molten metallic, and the sky seemed formed of the same dumb substance, the clouds dipping low to the land and brooding. Now, at shortly before eight in the morning, Jason gazed down at his pale, pajama-dressed arm that had swung out that day seemingly of its own volition, and he wondered whether it had been simply an unthinking moment of self-protection, the primitive part of the brain taking precedence in a moment of intense distress. Or was the culprit those distant fantasies of boyhood, the hero with the karate chop, the insistence that you never back down? Or perhaps memories of the clash of bodies on the football line, the masculine assaults of the legal brief, the invincibility of privilege? Ever since he had first awakened at the hospital following the surgery, when he was still in a fog of blood loss and painkillers, he had been playing out the different explanations and theories as an interior debate, interpreting and deconstructing the sudden violence of his forearm thrashing against the weapon—that forearm arriving, it seemed, with the simultaneity of the explosion and what he would imagine, later, as someone slamming the blunt end of a sledgehammer into his center mass.

"Do you need help to the bathroom before I go?" Marjorie asked.

Her hair had settled over the years into a distinguished yet somehow fierce gray, and she ran a brush through it before the full-length mirror on the interior of the closet door. A moment earlier he had studied, through the reflection, how she threaded her earrings into place.

"I'm fine," he said.

"At least let me help you stand."

"I said I'm fine."

"What's this martyr thing, Jay? It's silly."

"I thought I was supposed to do things on my own."

"I'm trying to help."

The bed sank as she sat down and then bent over to slip on her shoes—she had an obsession for Gucci—and he knew it was only a matter of a few brief moments before she would ask him if he wanted her to bring breakfast or coffee to the bed, if he needed her to slide the walker closer so he could grip it more easily, if she should fetch the remote for the television or grab his Kindle from the dresser, if he needed her to plug his cell phone into the charger before she left for work, if he'd had his morning medications, if he remembered that the nurse would arrive at shortly before eleven. Her tone as she spoke would be solicitous and patient, and only a few furtive glances at the alarm clock on the bedside table would betray any hint of impatience.

The thought was simply too much, he knew—given the current state of things between them—so he swung his legs from bed and reached out for the walker, drawing it closer, lifting himself to shuffle toward the en suite. His ribs and chest still felt as though he were butcher meat tied loosely together with string, and the pain was sometimes a deep throb and other times a sudden fire, but he pushed himself forward and closed the door with finality behind him.

Standing in front of the toilet was painful, but he refused to sit. As much as Jason was obsessed with reviewing the events of the shooting, he was also consumed with a memory of an exchange with his wife from a few weeks before. They had been out at their favorite Thai restaurant—Suan Nong Nooch—and they were both starting in on their curries—he liked the green, she the Massaman—when she informed him that she'd put in her papers for retirement, to begin on May 1. She had worked in the legal office for the city government for more than twenty-five years and was currently part of the team assigned directly to the mayor. That she wanted to retire with her pension was no surprise: she had been planning her exit for several years now, weighing the pros and cons, voicing her many dissatisfactions with the endemic problems facing the city. What was surprising was what Marjorie had said next, as casually as though wondering aloud if she would have room following the meal for mango sticky rice. She said, "I'm thinking about moving to Alamogordo. It would get me closer to the kids."

He remembered how much, at the time, the words had seemed a kind of puzzle. Was she suggesting spending part of the year in New Mexico and part with him in Chicago? Was she proposing that they maintain two homes together, one in each state, and fly back and forth when they could? Was she asking, indirectly, for a divorce, informing him that she didn't want to share with him any longer a life or a bed? The worst part, it had seemed, was how she seemed to assume that this was no big deal, that surely he must feel the same way, that retirement by definition meant couples in interminably long marriages flew off in their own separate directions.

"What are you saying?" he had asked.

She didn't seem to know. Again and again in the arguments that flared up over the days that followed this first quiet pronouncement, her position underwent unexpected swings and reversals. He was furious, of course, and more so—though this part he couldn't explain to himself—because she seemed so mercurial in the moods she kept directing his way. If she'd asked flat out to end the marriage he would have understood, but this vacillation seemed, somehow, more insulting. Of course she still loved him, she had said during one of their rows . . . she just wasn't certain she wanted to share with him every hour and day and year she might have left. She hadn't lived on her own since they first moved into an apartment together following law school. She hadn't been her own person, her own authentic agent.

"Authentic agent?" he had said, but she pretended not to hear the bite in his tone.

"And I want to see my grandson more often. Is that so hard to understand?"

"Of course not."

"I want to help raise him."

But it was more than that, too. She wanted a place of her own. No, she explained, she didn't want to share that space with him each time he came to visit. No, she didn't want to visit him in Chicago. Or maybe she did. How could she know in advance, until she'd had some time to herself, until she learned to breathe again through her own independent lungs?

It was infuriating, actually. Jason had somehow become, in this scenario, the patriarchal oppressor, the man refusing to allow the little lady to have her own existence, despite the fact of her own high-powered career and substantial income, despite the fact that, as near as he could recall, they had both long supported women's causes and women's rights, were liberal democrats despite the right-leaning or even reactionary beliefs of so many of their friends and corporate colleagues. He was one of *them* now, apparently, one of the ones who wanted to tell women what they could and could not do with their own lives and bodies, who believed that the differences in the sexes meant that certain limitations and restrictions were both resonable and fair, that to be a man meant lording over the fairer sex around you. Yes, it was all galling, and worse was the fact that Marjorie seemed dismayed by his surprise, as though this deficiency in their marital arrangement—the eternal yoke of matrimony—must surely be discernable to all.

After flushing the toilet, he made his way with the walker to the bedroom window. Lake Michigan, he always imagined, seemed more primitive in winter than in summer, more brooding and contemplative, more sober-minded, more raw and true to its nature. He preferred the winter vista, even the fog that clung to the shoreline some early mornings, drifting like a wraith into the city.

He tried to draw in a deep breath as he stood there, but those were the ones that always hurt now—an ice pick jabbed into the ribs or the muscle. He had no memory of the short trip to the hospital in the ambulance, no memory of the intensive care unit or being wheeled into surgery. Later, he was informed that the bullet had penetrated the chest, causing bleeding wounds on both the anterior and posterior walls of the left pulmonary artery. He was fortunate to be alive. He was fortunate that the 9mm bullet had missed several crucial thoracic cavity organs. He might easily have bled to death on the sidewalk, could have succumbed to any number of devastating outcomes during surgery, or to serious infection after the fact. So of course Marjorie wasn't saying anything more yet about her planned exodus to New Mexico. Neither of them had broached the topic even once, not while he was still recuperating in the hospital, not now that he was back home and on the arduous road—he'd been told—to full recovery. For now, she played the dramatic role of Florence Nightingale, dutiful and loving. She was the perfect wife—subjugated, she probably thought, by her husband's encounter with a bullet.

He made his way as best he could into the kitchen, where he poured himself a bowl of cereal and then got down to the serious business of swallowing his morning medications.

The nurse's name was Janice Satterfield, though the nametag she wore simply said JAN, all in caps: an announcement over a loudspeaker, adamant in forced friendliness. She was perhaps in her early to middle thirties, with short blond hair and a single purple streak on the right side, not rebellious so much as festive, a playful wink to the unconventional. She was wide at the hips and a talker, free with information about her own life. This included about her deeply flawed live-in boyfriend, who apparently had recently lost his job as a welder and simply moped around the apartment all day, good for nothing, then wanted her to go out drinking with him or partying every night to all hours, and pay for them both. Her face was pretty, her laugh infectious, her youth enviable, and Jason couldn't help himself: each day before her arrival, and despite whatever pain it might cause, he made certain to shave and to slick back his hair, to drag on a nice pair of slacks and a button-down dress shirt, to wear clean socks and polished shoes, to gargle with mouthwash, and to leave strategically where he'd been resting on the living-room couch an impressive stack of legal papers or heavy tomes—Tolstoy or Melville or Eliot. All this was foolish, of course, vain and petty, but there it was. It was bad enough to feel as helpless as a child, worse when she spoke loudly as though she suspected the onset of deafness or maybe dementia. She checked his wound, took his temperature and blood pressure, asked him questions, and engaged him in simple forms of physical therapy. She always seemed a little bored, with a kind of patient professionalism that somehow deflated him.

He crossed to the door on this day in response to the buzzer, and when she was there beside him in the condominium, when he was back on the bed and she was stripping off the old bandage, he sucked in his belly just enough to diminish the slope of the sag.

"It smells like snow is coming," she said.

"What smell is that?"

"It's hard to describe."

Her fingers were at work by then, touching the uncovered skin, not unlike when a woman or a man cut his hair and he felt the fingers against his scalp or his neck, not unlike when the dental hygienist slipped her or his fingers far into the moist mouth, not unlike the chiropractor bending and cracking the body. It was a forced intimacy, professional yet nonetheless awkward, and Jan's scent as she leaned near seemed a fusion of coconut shampoo and aloe lotion and salty sweat.

One of his earliest and fondest memories of his wife was when, during their first year of living together, before they married, they drove out from the city into the northern regions of the state, then across the border into Wisconsin. One of the partners at the law firm where they were both associates—newly minted to the profession—owned a cabin on a private lake south and west of the Wisconsin Dells, in the middle of nowhere. They passed a long weekend looking out at the green-blue eye of the lake, they took the rowboat into the gentle waters, and they swam naked from the wooden dock and then made love in the cabin—and once right there by the shore, their bodies redolent with loamy lake smells, the sky above fevered with sun. They were not normally the type to enjoy roughing it, but the sounds of the birds and the tree frogs and the bullfrogs and the crickets late at night were a kind of lullaby, and the paths that wound up into the woods carried them into a land where they saw no one but themselves, where they could carry the newness of their love up to a sloping ridge that looked out at both the cabin and the lake, and from which they could talk about their childhoods and their future plans as though, in such serenity, it were truly possible to lay out the blueprint of your life, to construct it from whatever pieces you might desire. Marjorie's hair was still long and crow black in those days—and, unlike when she tied it back for work, she wore it loosely around her shoulders. One morning when they climbed from the lake he saw a leech clinging to his ankle, swelling fat with blood, and she removed it gently with tweezers she kept in her purse. They lay beneath the patience of the sun, and this was their life.

He was dozing when Marjorie returned home in the early evening, but still he heard the latch of the door, heard her footsteps on the carpeting, heard her speaking in a soft voice to one or both of the cats, then sensed her standing in the bedroom doorway and gazing down at him. Her presence was a weight, and so he kept his eyes closed, his back turned to the door. Had he been dreaming just now about that lake? Had his earlier thoughts followed him down into his sleep? What was its name? Lake Gilbert? Lake Gilliam? Something like that. He suspected that Marjorie would remember—she had that knack for distant details—and one part of him wanted to roll over to ask her, to tell her what thoughts had consumed him for much of the day, to remind her how, one night by that lake, they had built a fire and attempted to warm baked beans above the flames. They had forgotten, though, to poke a hole first in the can's top, and the explosion had sent it six feet into the air, spilling beans everywhere around them. They were lucky not to have been impaled with shrapnel. But they had been happy then, hadn't they? Couldn't you almost imagine the happiness from those days as something tangible, visceral, something you carried inside your body as much as you carried the scaffolding of your own bones? He wanted to tell her that, wanted to ask if she thought that happiness of that sort could hide inside the body for decades, only to be discovered once again, returned to the surface, nurtured? He wanted to ask her not to go to New Mexico, not to abandon this life they had built, this love—if that was what it should be called—that they had tended like a garden through what, for both of them now, was the majority of their lives. This was who they were, after all. This was what they had made, for good or for ill. The words were on his lips, perched there, waiting.

He rolled over and saw her closer than he'd expected, a few feet from the bed, gazing down at him, her eyes narrowing with concern.

He didn't know what words would escape from his mouth until they slipped into the air. He said, "What the hell? I'm trying to sleep."

She turned on her heels and left the room.

It was late spring, less than two weeks before Marjorie was set to leave from O'Hare airport to Alamogordo, New Mexico. They were sitting near the main entrance of Suan Nong Nooch—

after a long day of work for both of them—waiting for their carryout order to be ready. They were sitting side by side but checking messages on their phones, thumb-typing their replies. They'd come to an understanding of sorts. Marjorie would rent month-to-month at first, and the two of them would gauge together the pros and cons of life apart. It would be civilized and supportive, and they would speak often by phone, and he could come out to visit every few months, both to see her and to see their children and the grandchild. They would not call it a separation, would not call it a precursor to divorce. They had decided not to call it anything at all—especially to their son and daughter—but to leave it nameless, amorphous, a drifting cloud that could be anything, then something else a moment later.

Jason peered up when a couple standing near the door—apparently also waiting for a carryout order—began to argue in low voices. They were young, perhaps in their early twenties but appearing even more youthful than that, and the girl had orange-red hair and a pretty figure and an earnest face, and the young man reminded Jason faintly of the boy by the Clark Street Bridge, all skin and bones, a child's mouth and eyes.

Ever since the shooting, Jason had thought he'd seen the assailant everywhere he went on the streets. The boy would be coming toward him in a throng of pedestrians, or peering out a bus window, or smoking in an alley. But this young man in the restaurant did bear an uncanny resemblance, though he was older, like a more mature sibling. At the sight of him Jason felt a sudden thrum of pain where the bullet had entered his body.

Often, before showering in the mornings, Jason would stand before the mirror and marvel at the pucker scar where the projectile had burrowed into the waiting cave, had hibernated there until the surgeon had dug it free. And he studied the surgical scars as well, tracing a finger over where the scalpel had peeled him back and opened the secrets of his body for all to see.

The young man had closed his eyes and was shaking his head. His Adam's apple, like that of the boy with the gun, protruded and bobbed in his throat. The young woman was clearly furious now. She wore red lipstick—too much of it, too bright—and her mouth appeared like a wound as she berated the young man for something he had done, though the din in the restaurant—the clink of plates and silverware, the white blurring sound of the voices—made it impossible to snare the words and piece them into something coherent. All that was clear was that the girl began poking one slender finger into the young man's chest, stabbing and stabbing, and then the boy's eyes came open and there was a downturned sneer at one side of his mouth, a dismissive impatience, and he reached out with two hands and pressed them to the girl's chest, pressed them either just above her breasts or perhaps directly on them, and shoved, his arms extending the way the boy's arm had extended with the handgun. The girl went stumbling backwards, nearly falling. The shove was violent, final, and the young man crossed his arms over his chest and closed his eyes again, as though slipping back into a world outside of this one. He wore a faint hint of a mustache, though maybe he simply hadn't shaved for a few days, and there was something sallow in his expression, something cold.

At once, without knowing he intended it, Jason was on his feet. Perhaps he meant to cross the room and assist the young woman in regaining her balance. Or perhaps he meant to charge toward the young man and give him the dressing-down he so clearly deserved, grip him by the fabric of his Minnesota

Twins sweatshirt, lecture him about decency and respect, bring his own face, if need be, within a few inches of the boy's face, and let him know once and for all what was and was not acceptable. A fury gripped Jason, held him in its thrall, and he was already breathless from it, already overflowing.

Suddenly Marjorie's hand gripped his forearm tightly and yanked him. He swiveled and was met by the general import of her expression, the unambiguous implications around the mouth and eyes. And he could see, beyond his wife, outside the restaurant window, spring rain beginning to fall, dropping from the Chicago sky, smearing the glass and dripping from the eaves. He was a fool now, a joke. Apparently there was no longer any course of action that provided even a modicum of dignity. If he sat there on his hands, he was ineffectual, passive, irrelevant. If he rose and challenged the young man, he was a buffoon from another century, a barbarian. This was what his life was now, it seemed. And from the edges of his peripheral vision, he saw that the young woman had returned to the side of the young man, whose eyes were open now. His arm was curled around her shoulder, his skinny hand dangling toward the center of her body, where she gripped it with both of her own hands, the freckles on her youthful face an indecipherable maze, her long hair a veil around her, a cloak.

"Sit down," his wife said.

He did.

Omens

THERE WAS SOMETHING ABOUT THE WAY THEIR LEGS DANGLED that made the girls feel airborne. The train bridge was busy stretching itself across the river, and Wallace River was busy stretching itself through the trees, gray and in a hurry. And the girls, puffy eyed in the raw newness of morning, were talking in low voices and holding onto the railing and occasionally leaning over to spit, then watching the drops fall like wet missiles.

Both girls were thirteen. Evie was the taller of the two, so skinny she sometimes felt awkward in her own body, like she'd been forced into it, while Abby had a hive of freckles on her nose and orange hair that got her teased on occasion. Both girls were dressed alike in T-shirts and shorts and flip-flops, though the flip-flops were behind them now on the tracks, the girls' bare feet making twirling motions—their legs might have been stirring a great pot.

Suddenly a crow levitated above the trees, and both girls looked in that direction. Evie thought the sounds the crow made were like a ghost calling out in a dream, and Abby thought the body of the bird might have been a dark boatmoving across the sky's bright sea, and both girls—best friends since third grade—found themselves thinking in that moment about Abby's brother.

Later they climbed down from the bridge and waded two steps into the river. Liquid hands pushed against their ankles and calves. The current spoke in a loud and trickling voice.

When they sloshed back out, Evie said, "Remember him yelling that time? For going in his room while he was sleeping?"

Abby, pushing her wet feet into her flip-flops, said nothing.

Evie gave her a nudge. "Did we want him to watch cartoons with us? Is that it? How old were we anyway?"

"We should get back," Abby said.

"Eight? I guess it could have been nine."

"Stop," Abby said with just enough barb that both girls stopped talking and leaned their bodies into the steep hill leading out of the September coolness of the ravine and back up into the warmer terrain of the train tracks.

French toast sizzled and spat in a dark skillet. There were soy-sausage links too. Abby's mom held the spatula in her right hand, holding it in the air like a conductor.

The sight was weirdly familiar to Evie. Years of sitting at this same table in this same house on an early morning after she'd stayed the night, Abby's mom fixing breakfast and maybe asking about school or teasing them for being gigglers or complaining how they'd stayed up hopelessly late and had made too much noise, like the wild creatures they were. It was different now. Everything was. Everything looked the same on the outside but was different in its interior, like an apple that opens up into the ruined brown.

Evie glanced at Abby's mom as she placed the plates on the table. Mrs. Moran seemed like herself and not herself. It was something around her eyes. Something drooping at the corners of her mouth.

"Where did you girls get off to this morning?" she asked.

"You know," Evie said, giving the words a twist, "meeting boys and things by the river."

"Skinny-dipping," Abby said. "Their idea."

The joke had the old ring to it, as familiar as summer grass, and all three tried to grin to acknowledge that fact. Yet it seemed like there were fissures in the air. Loose things. Weak scaffoldings.

Mrs. Moran brushed hair from her face with the back of a hand. She said, "You girls aren't supposed to be getting up at first light anymore. You're teenagers now. You're supposed to annoy me and Abby's dad by sleeping till noon."

"That's how eager we were to see those naked boys," Abby said.

Evie had just poured the syrup and now licked some off the side of her thumb. "We just walked down to the train bridge," she said. "That's all."

"Okay," Abby's mom said. "You girls want orange juice?"

Abby's dad came walking in at that moment, opened the refrigerator and bent into it, an act so normal in its execution that for a moment Evie felt herself wanting to cry, a feeling that grew even stronger when breakfast was over and she and Abby climbed the stairs to Abby's room and went past Jack's closed door. That door, now, seemed like something that opened into a deep cave or a dark well. Evie could never look at it without sinking inside herself, drooping in her lungs enough that breathing became a strain.

"What do you want to do?" Abby asked once they were back sitting on her bed.

"Where are those boys we were talking about?" Evie teased.

"Maybe they're there now. They might have been running a little late."

"I guess we could go see," Evie said.

"In other words," Abby said, "we'll go back and spit some more off the bridge."

It wasn't until after the ride home from Abby's after lunch, feeling sleepy in the Camry as her mom drove, that Evie let the bumps on old Highway 17 rock her into an almost stuporous state. In the past, she'd always felt like only half herself whenever Abby wasn't around, but since July that had changed. Now, in Abby's presence, it sometimes felt like the world was off its axis. She thought of Jack's door at the top of the stairs, right next to the shared bathroom, and she thought of a dream she'd had one night not long after the funeral. In life she'd never thought of Jack as anything but Abby's weird older brother, but in death he'd been altered. He came toward her in the dream, touched her shoulder, and actually bent down to kiss her. It was so startling that she backed away quickly. She wanted to tell him he was dead, but it seemed a rude thing to say, and she didn't know in any case why being dead should make him want to kiss her. That was when she woke from the dream.

"Don't forget you've got your eye appointment after school tomorrow," her mom said now in the car. "Don't take the bus. I'll be leaving work early to come get you."

"Mom," Evie said, her tongue feeling heavy and lethargic.

Her mom said, "Didn't you get any sleep at all? I swear, you two do the same thing every time."

Evie said, "Everything's wrong now. It just is."

"What are you talking about?"

"You know," Evie said.

"Oh."

"So don't get on me about being sleepy."

Evie sat up straight. And in that moment, she saw something at the side of the road—they were on the outskirts of town, close to the Fairgrounds. Three turkey vultures were perched in a tree. They had their blood-red little heads. They had their shrouds for wings. They sat there, as still as statuary. It seemed to Evie in that moment like a terrible sign, like something trying to warn her or maybe brand her, and the panic blossomed in her belly and chest.

She swiveled and faced her shoulders toward the window. The vultures were gone now and the car was coming up on Adventure Skating and Putt Putt. Then, after that, the Dairy Queen. They were almost in the thick of it now, and Evie watched the world blurring by, strobing into existence then out, all of it in a hurry, and then they came to the first stoplight, which was red, and everything stopped.

Her eyes felt funny the next day. They stung and teared. Evie was back in her mom's car, this time on the way through downtown. Her mom's voice was a hive inside the enclosed space, a buzz of questions and remarks and the occasional cough. Evie wore a plastic film across her eyes—to dim the world from the drops she'd had.

She startled her mom by clawing at her arm suddenly and saying, "Pull in. Right there. Before you pass it."

"What?" her mom asked.

"I want to visit Jack," Evie said.

Her mom hit the brakes while peering in the rearview mirror, and then they were veering into the cemetery, the tires making a small wail of complaint. Soon they were out of the car in the afternoon wind, which tried to yank the plastic glasses from Evie's eyes. She held them in place while she and her mom walked amid the graves, which seemed both solemn and a little creepy to Evie, especially since everything was green from the glasses, like seeing it all from the bottom of a swimming pool.

"You know where the marker is?" her mom asked.

"Wait here," Evie said. "I want to stand there by myself."

And so she did. The wind snapped her blouse around her body. It was a warmish wind and intrusive. The name was right there, carved into the stone with a stark permanence: *Jackson Wallace Doran II*. Below his name, the years were laid out like a sad blueprint or map, something with clear and lasting demarcations on either side. Evie stood there amid the dead, all of them hidden in their privacy beneath the ground. She recalled standing there on the day of the funeral itself, the heavy heat giving way at one point to such a sudden and brief spatter of a shower that it hadn't quite seemed real, the sky letting a couple of warm drops slip away but then clamping down and restraining itself.

Back in the car, Evie asked her mom, "Did you see those vultures yesterday? On the way back from Abby's house?"

"What?" her mom asked.

"In a tree by the road. A little before we got to Dairy Queen."

"I don't remember," her mom said. "How come?"

"There must have been something like that for Jack. You know, in the days leading up. To warn him."

Her mom put out her cigarette in the ashtray. Smoke—it looked green to Evie—snaked through the car and bumped against the car roof. Her mom said, "You don't believe that sort of thing."

"I know," Evie said, "but still. If he'd seen those vultures like I did, maybe it would have made him watch closer what he was doing. He would have seen the car coming. Gotten off the bike."

Her mom looked at her instead of at the road. "Evie," she said, "it doesn't help to think that way. *If only* isn't a game worth playing. Okay?"

Evie considered that. It felt like she was chewing on the thoughts, working them down to something digestible. Then she said, "The driver should have been going slower."

"Sure," her mom said. "But you know, of course, that the woman said Jack seemed to hit a bump or something and started swerving."

"It's just not right," Evie said.

"You've got a point there."

Evie tore off her flimsy little sunglasses and left them in a heap in her lap. Her eyes stung against the light, but she refused to squint.

At lunch the next day, Abby and Evie were sitting near the trash bins as usual, complaining about how the shepherd's pie was maybe made of actual shepherds or German shepherds, when Evie told Abby about visiting Jack's grave.

"What?" Abby said, half-choking on a bite.

"On the way back from my eye appointment."

"Why?" Abby asked.

"We were driving by. I wanted to. Why do you sound mad?"

Abby pushed away her plastic tray. It bumped Evie's tray,

like it had hard feelings. Abby said, "Why are you telling me about it?"

"I don't know."

"Well, don't. I don't want to hear it."

"I feel bad, Abby," Evie said. "That's all."

Now Abby's voice was raised, lifting and flying across the cafeteria, drawing eyes their direction. "Well, aren't you so noble, Evie. I wish I could be half as noble as you. The whole world does."

"What's going on?"

"I guess you need to give us lessons in how to feel bad. Maybe I should take notes. Do you want to tell it again?"

"Why are you yelling?"

"Because," Abby said, leaping up. Whenever she got worked up like this, her whole face turned a deep and insistent crimson, like the last of a day's sunlight suffusing a cloud.

"I'm sorry," Evie said. "I didn't mean anything."

"Oh, I'm sure you didn't," Abby said, still standing, perched like she was about to storm off. "You never do. You just don't get it. You bringing up Jack all the time makes it worse. Get it through your skull. It's not helping."

Evie didn't realize she was crying until a warm drop splatted on the back of her hand. She made a sniffling sound then coughed, choking on her own woe. She said, "I never meant anything bad. I'm sorry, Ab. I'm so sorry. That's the truth. You know it is."

Abby sat back down. Of course she did. And both of them were breathing heavily. Great heaves of it there in the cafeteria. And soon they both started eating again, their heads hunched down toward their plates. Tiny little bites. And then they started talking in soft voices about algebra and Ms. Katz. How she actually looked a little like a cat. And how stupid algebra was. And how they both were pretty sure they were going to flunk the quiz that afternoon. And their words felt like some kind of gauze in the air around them. And now and then they gave each other "sorry" glances. And one thing was certain and inviolable, despite everything: they were best friends and had to be forever.

Friday night at Evie's house, the girls watched Netflix. They were in the living room with the lights out, Evie's laptop conjuring flashing images and sounds about pretend lives in miniature. They munched from a Cheez-It bag and drank Sprite and ragged about girls from their school and mentioned boys they used to like and maybe still did—sort of—and berated characters on the screen for their stupid life choices. And Evie made certain not to mention Jack—except once quickly in passing. But the next noon when Abby's mom pulled up the driveway and called Abby on her cell phone, both girls hurried out the front door and climbed in, heading back to the Doran house, at Abby's request.

"There's something we need to do," she said.

And after Abby's parents left around two to play tennis at the public park—the girls found sports of any kind unfathomable—Abby asked Evie to follow her out the kitchen door.

"Why?" Evie asked.

"Just do it—please. For once, I don't want to talk about it."

There were three bikes leaning up against the shed past the vegetable garden, and Abby peeled away the top one and pushed it toward Evie, then selected one for herself. Soon they were riding down the gravel drive, which made for unsteady going, and then they were out on the road, neither of them with helmets on their heads, which made Evie uneasy. She would have said something if not for the fact that Abby seemed so somber and purposeful in the hard motion of her legs, like she was heading out on a great journey that required reverent silence—and maybe some kind of angry concentration.

It wasn't until they turned west on Old Decker Highway that Evie figured out where they were headed. It was a warm day but not hot, the air swirling around them as they pumped their legs, both of them breathing heavily from the effort. There weren't many cars, but the ones whooshing by were in a hurry, the sound unsettling, especially when a furniture truck hurtled past with the fat insistence of its rickety body. Abby still wasn't speaking, and Evie had a sudden image of the two of them riding out to the very edges of the globe, round and round the world until the centrifugal force of it pressed them harder and harder against the ground.

That was when she saw a white belly and a white rump bright in the glare of the afternoon. Just up ahead off the road. The poor deer was a small one, its dark eyes glassy and emptied, flies lifting like some strange symphony of sorrowful motion. Then the girls were past the dead creature, but Evie kept glancing back, wishing now even more that she had a helmet on, that she'd said something about it to Abby before they'd left. And she wished they weren't on this road where cars and trucks went past with no regard for their speed, Abby's hair a wild orange flag that was snapping. It seemed to Evie that a dead doe was a bad sign. Something to pay attention to. And the next car that sidled up close as it went by sent Evie into a small panic. What if it clipped them going past? What if they lost control like Jack had? But nothing happened. The car made a wide berth around them then sped off.

The spot, when they arrived, was marked with dirty old plastic flowers and a mangy wreath and a cross. It was depressing. There was nothing special about the place—just one more dot on the long continuum of farm fields and farmhouses and empty spaces. They were near Camden Road, which led, Evie knew, to Eric Redshaw's house, where Jack had been heading. One of the photos left beside the wreath was actually of Jack and Eric and two other friends, taken at Strikes Bowling, the rows of pins behind them on the lanes. Evie stared at the photo after she and Abby climbed off the bikes and stood before the whole sad display. To someone going by and looking out of their peripheral vision, it probably seemed like nothing more than road trash.

Abby still wasn't talking—it was getting a little uncomfortable—and suddenly she reached into her sweatshirt pocket and drew out what looked at first like a cigarette but was actually a little smaller and was twirled closed on both ends.

"Abby!" Evie said. "Where did you get that?"

"Colton Snyder," Abby said. "When I told him why, he gave it for free."

Then Abby was kneeling and hiding what she held beneath the wreath, giving the wreath afterwards a little pat like she was offering it a holy blessing in a church. Then she was up again and turning toward Evie, saying, "I wanted there to be at least one thing here he would like."

Evie giggled—it was true—but the laugh ended when Abby gave her a long and disapproving look. She said, "I brought you here so we could say goodbye to Jack together, Evie. But this is it. You hear me? We say goodbye then never mention him again."

"Are you serious?" Evie asked.

"I am."

"We're supposed to forget all about him?"

"Of course not. But it disrespects him to keep putting it into words."

"Why? I can't do it, Ab. How can you?"

Abby's next words arrived in the air like the bringing down of a lid. She said, "You'll do it if you want us to stay friends."

Then they were back on their bikes and riding the return route to Abby's house, though they stopped before arriving so they could leave the bikes and walk out again on the train bridge, where they sat with their legs dangling in that open space. Abby drew out another one of those little cigarettes and said, "Colton felt so bad he gave me two. Have you been thinking about what I said? You agree?"

"It doesn't seem right," Evie said.

"It does. It's the only thing that's seems right—the only thing since it happened."

"It's betraying him."

"No. The opposite."

"I can't. You can't mean it."

Abby said, "We'll smoke it as our final goodbye. If you can't do it, just go. Call your mom to come get you. I'm not kidding."

"Ab."

"Decide. Decide now."

"Ab."

"Then go, Evie. Just go. I'm not giving in on this."

Evie sucked in a hard breath then said, "Okay—I'll do it. Okay."

Abby lit the match and then the smell was around them. Both of them had tried it only once before—at that very same Colton Snyder's house—but this time the smoke seeped down into their lungs with a harsh reverence that made them both cough but not give up. Wallace River, beneath them, was heading out, hurrying on with its own concerns and imperatives, and the sky above them had its own private freight train of clouds.

At one point, the girls heard a horn in the distance, which startled them enough they both twitched, which made them laugh hysterically and in unison. But soon Evie looked away so Abby wouldn't see that she was crying some. She looked into the trees that were blurring green, and the thought occurred to her that she would carry the silence always in her chest or her throat, carry it in Abby's presence, carry it like weeds that keep growing in a field till they take over. She wanted to explain that to Abby, wanted to explain that it would always be waiting there between them, always lurking, always watching them and passing judgment, but then Abby was on her feet so Evie rose too. They moved ahead on wobbly legs, making their way back to the bikes, and rode unsteadily the rest of the way down the road then up the gravel driveway, leaning the bikes back against the shed.

The world around them, as they started toward the house, seemed soft around its edges, like it might start blinking on and off like a firefly in a backyard on a hot summer night. The sun was dipping down into the trees, lingering there like it might get stuck. And the girls walked arm and arm into the house.

II.

Snow Crow

AND THE DAYS WERE MADE OF AUGURIES. AND THE CRICKET calls arrived disembodied from the field. And a dead mole lay on its back by the garage, gathering its thin blanket of ants. And wasps hummed outside the boy's window like primitive wraiths. And one morning, he found a dead crow in the woods and carried it back to the house, hiding it at the back of his closet like a reliquary. And sometimes he imagined the creature calling to him in the night, calling to him in his dreams, and the boy would rise, pull the string for the closet light, and open the cardboard box. And there was the crow: its dark wings motionless, its dark and lacquered eyes gazing up at him. And sometimes in the mornings, the boy stepped into the backyard and gazed at the sun with its raw, sepulchral eye. And at breakfast, now and then, he asked about his father. And his mother would cross her arms over her chest or set his plate so forcefully on the table that the boy would look away. And some afternoons, he sat in his closet and imagined the crow lifting itself on the dark oars of its wings, rowing high above the trees. Or the boy imagined a crow call fissuring the air, a crow call that was both corporeal and incorporeal at once. And the smell in the boy's closet was like something secretive congealing on the surface of a pond. And on the evening when the first light snow of the season came dropping toward the land, the boy carried the crow back into the woods and tossed it as high as he could manage into the air.

Occultations

THEY FELL IN LOVE LIKE THISTLE WEEDS. LIKE BANEBERRIES. Like calamus. And they imagined that their bodies were like a mud river whispering in the night as it slipped past. Like someone had drowned there and was forever bobbing in the current. Often they held hands and kissed and gripped each other and refused to let go. Their hands were pennyworts and checkerberries. Their hands were an offering of feverfew and skullcaps and bittersweets. And at night when they shared a bed, they were reminded of frostweed and darting bats and albino moons. Sometimes they believed that their breaths were occultations, that their hands were transforming into blossoms and claws. And the lovers fought some nights like chorus frogs or starving dogs. Other times they were as silent as the pale and translucent skin of the stars. And come morning, they hissed at each other like snakes and held each other like epileptic grass twitching in the wind. And when they were together, that wind howled and the carrion flies hovered. And when they were apart, the sky was a dim cloth and their memories were brackishly alluring ponds. And then, come winter, the snow fell around them like pale ash.

Rune

THE WINTER AFTER HIS BROTHER DROWNS, THE BOY SEES HIS father carrying a deer out from the woods. He is carrying the deer on his shoulders. And the boy imagines that his brother is the blood that drips from the deer onto the snow, that his brother is the four legs that droop in the way the boy's own legs droop on the nights when his father carries him on his shoulders up to bed. Or maybe his brother is the snow that falls into the deer's open eyes, which are lacquered black. Or maybe his brother is the moonlight after dark or the shadow of a winter crow on the dead grass or the way the days blink on and off like summer fireflies. And sometimes after dark, the boy stands at his bedroom window and peers down in the direction of the river where his brother drowned, and the moon above that river reminds him of a bone buried in the sky's mud. The stars above that river are scattered like thrown bones. Sometimes the boy hears the voices of his parents arguing in the walls, and sometimes the boy wakes to those voices and imagines for a moment that his brother is there in the room with him, that his brother is asleep in his bed. And the boy's breaths feel like something hollowed out. And the nights remind the boy of the way squirrels fall from tree limbs each time his father takes him into the woods and pulls the trigger on his .22, the slack weights dropping through the air before the creatures bounce on the ground. And the boy imagines that the severed heads of those squirrels on the kitchen counter are his brother, and his brother is gazing at him with forlorn eyes. The boy imagines that those severed heads arrange themselves like runes. Later, when the boy sneaks out the kitchen door, he notices how shadows bisect the yard and dead leaves shuffle primitively beneath him as he follows the deer path toward the river. And the boy listens to the language of those leaves beneath him, leaves that whisper in the secret voice of his brother. Somehow that language seems older than the clouds or the moon or the stars. The boy stands by the river where, in summer, the minnows in the shallows will be shadow ghosts. And those ghosts, when the warmer weather arrives, will be his brother. The boy leans against a winter tree and wonders how it holds itself in place for so long, remains motionless as the planet turns and the years accumulate like falling snow. And the boy knows that the dead tree is his brother. The boy leans against it and studies the frozen river that holds its breath, and that held breath must be what his brother dreams, and the skin of the snow atop the river is also what his brother dreams, and the day breathes in and out like pale clouds.

Feral Prophecy

SHE HAS JUST PASSED THE FIVE-MONTH MARK, THE SAME AS two years earlier. So he gathers fleabane and white snakeroot in the July heat, ties them together with horsehair, and hides them beneath their bed. That night, while his wife breathes softly and occasionally rolls over, he lies awake and thinks about how pale and weak the moon looks outside their bedroom window, a skull buried in the sky's mud. And in the morning, he watches a hawk skimming low to the field behind the barn, watches it gently lift a mouse into the air then ferry it away. His wife tells him over breakfast that Septoria blight has laid waste again to her tomato plants. She tells him that a wasp with its black tripartite body stung her in the neck as she walked back from fetching the newspaper. And his wife is sick to her stomach after breakfast. So later he gathers bull thistle and black cohosh, fastens them with a dead garter snake, and hides them beneath her dresser. And he dreams that night that her belly swells and swells, that their child grows larger and larger inside the alluvium of her body, swimming in its enclosed salt sea. And the next morning he gathers oxeye daisies and sourwood, ties them together with wild grass, jabs his thumb to spill three bright red drops, and hides the flowers beneath the crib beside the window. Then he stands and gazes for a moment at the crib. For he can never look at it now without remembering when he first put it up two years earlier, without remembering how he quickly took it back down. And that night he dreams that their child curls in his wife's belly like a sleeping snake, curls into the ouroboros, flourishing like wildflowers inside the body's loam. And when his wife wakes in the morning, he grips her in his arms and says, *It's wild this time. Strong*. And he holds his wife so tightly in his arms that she whispers damply in his ear that she can't breathe.

III.

Migration

ONE OF ETHAN'S EARLY MEMORIES IS OF STANDING BEFORE A house like a big white cake and holding a clipboard in his arms. It must be summer because the sun is a bright lozenge in the sky, and he is pretty sure it is still Ohio, and it is a fancy neighborhood with big houses and even bigger lawns. Even the door bell sounds fancy when he rings it.

And when the door swings inward, there is a woman with a cigarette in the corner of her mouth and smoke curling past her eyes and making her squint as she glances over him toward his dad's car at the curb, and she says, Can I help you?

Leukemia, Ethan says, knowing he isn't supposed to start with that but can't remember the rest of it.

What? the woman asks.

We're selling cookies, Ethan says. You might know her. Taylor Haggerty. She goes to my school. It's a bake sale. For the family.

Oh dear, the woman says.

My mom bakes the cookies, he says. He knows he is mangling things but adds, Chocolate chip or peanut butter. I think there was another one too. It goes for the doctors. Did I say her name yet?

The woman says, My Deidre is in 4th grade. What grade are you in?

Ethan's face feels like he's leaning too close to a fire. He says, We can't take checks.

Oh, the woman says.

Ten dollars for a dozen. Twenty for three dozen. We deliver in a week. I have a speech I was supposed to give.

When the woman smiles, her silver necklace shimmers in that glaring sun, like fish shimmering in water. She says, I guess I could help out. How does it work?

Ethan looks at his clipboard. He knows he is supposed to write something. The page is already half filled with pretend names. He says, You give me money.

But mostly he remembers being on the road and waking in the car some mornings in the dim gray while geese slip past above the trees with their ghostly squawking, and his dad is saying they have the right idea to flap their wings and skedaddle somewhere warmer. And in his memory he sees his father cooking baked beans over an outside fire and hears him complaining about his former boss, how he used to have a soul but lost it. And he remembers missing his mother and his dad once breaking a window with a brick at a house on a lake, the kind, his dad explains, rich people leave unattended. And the house has heat and toilets and running water, and Ethan eats crackers and stands before the high windows at the back and imagines living there forever and dreams some nights that his mother's hair is like cobwebs in his face. And sometimes at restaurants, his dad says, Just get up and walk out when I give you a nod.

And one night they park beneath a bridge, and Ethan wakes to feel the car shaking, and he was dreaming about their old house, but the dream slips away the moment his eyes come open, and a train is going by, and the noise seems to last forever, and he has to pee but doesn't want to wake his dad, and on the road the next morning his father says, We're nomads now.

And they drive and drive, and the car is where they live, and Ethan feels the motion of the road beneath the tires, and it's a raft on a river that won't end, and in a dream one night he imagines his mother on the other side of a door and not sick anymore and knocking lightly so he knows she is there.

And sometimes Ethan imagines that his father is a bear. His father is big. His father has hair on his back and his chest. And in the boy's memory, his father is also like the crows they hear calling sometimes when they sleep or cook outside. And Ethan imagines that one of those black bodies oaring above the trees must surely be his dad, even though his dad is there beside him. Or maybe his dad is chimney smoke or a coyote they see once with only three legs, or maybe his father is the memory of snow from when they lived in Ohio, and sometimes his dad changes up the story so it's not leukemia but new uniforms for a school basketball team. But mostly it's leukemia.

And in Florida, near Orlando, they stop one afternoon at a house that is not white but bright yellow, bright like the sun in a painting. And the man who answers is even bigger than Ethan's dad, even more like a bear.

We have chocolate chip or peanut butter or sugar cookies, Ethan says.

You said you go to school around here? the man asks. Which one?

She has leukemia, Ethan says. It costs a lot of money. She can die.

A little girl stands behind her dad's legs. She looks maybe seven. Her face collapses, and she grips her dad's leg harder.

Ethan leans toward her and says, I just say that so we get the money. It's all pretend.

The dad's voice is raised when he confronts Ethan's dad at the car. He shouts something about calling the police. He slaps the hood. Then Ethan's dad gets mad as they drive away, and he yells at Ethan, and Ethan draws air into his lungs and holds it there like something he means to horde inside him forever.

And his best friend outside of Tampa is nicknamed Grub. And Grub lives in the same trailer park where Ethan and his dad stay with his dad's younger brother and girlfriend. And sometimes Ethan and Grub walk to the Dairy Queen, and the days are like the throwing of bones, and there is a certain albino quality to Grub's skin, and he is at least two inches shorter than Ethan, and they spend the summer in a kind of expansive idleness, watching television or listening to Grub's older brother, Caleb, who talks all the time with Debbie and Doris McCarthy, sisters from a trailer near the landfill. And Caleb leaves crude remarks in chalk on the street outside the trailer where the sisters live, and the sisters give him the finger and laugh.

Then one boiling afternoon while Ethan and Caleb are taking turns on Caleb's trampoline and Grub is watching, Caleb says to his brother, Better not lean against that post, Grub. A kid was struck by lightning in that exact same spot.

And Debbie, sitting on the dead grass, says, All that was left was his shoes.

And Grub leaps away so quickly—clearly terrified—that it becomes the summer's joke. If they see a dead ant on the ground, they say, Oh my God, Grub, that's a terrible sign. It means you'll die.

And another day when they see a dead bird on the road, Caleb dips a stick beneath the corpse and flings it toward Grub so it lands on his shoe.

If it touched you you're dead, Caleb says. We're really sorry, but that's how it works.

And Ethan tries his best those days to walk small, tries to keep Caleb and Debbie and Doris from tossing a dead bird toward him as well, and he does his best to laugh and join in when Grub is being ridiculed, and by fall Ethan and his dad are far away in Texas and Ethan misses Grub terribly and knows he was his best friend ever, but he and his dad are back in the car so often it seems like nothing exists except the unspooling road.

And at one house the doorbell has a cheerful song, and the woman who answers scowls, and she is not his mom, and he realizes he hasn't thought about his mother for a long while.

And he grips his clipboard and opens his mouth to speak, but the woman says, We're not interested.

And it's Indiana where Ethan turns fourteen, and they live in a tiny cabin on Hog Creek, and his dad has a summer job as a roofer, and it seems the creek has a lot to say because it's always talking, even to the moonlight at night. And Ethan hears that voice inside his sleep, as though there is a membrane through which the language slips. And some days he stands by the bank and peers down at the muddy current that always heads out in the same direction, and there is a worn deer path in the woods that leads to Paige's house. But it's not there where they meet. They meet by the creek and look down at the torsional movements of the tiny, silver fish. And Paige is short and sturdy, and they sit on fallen logs and hold hands and sometimes kiss or look down at the gray or brown smear of the water. And Paige talks about how much her parents' voices are always angry drums inside their house, and her legs sometimes dangle from a log and twitch like they forget how to stay still.

And Ethan talks about being on the road so much in the past while his father gripped two hands on the steering wheel and gazed at the asphalt for what seemed like hours, all without blinking. And later, in Michigan, he sleeps with a girl for the first time. Her name is Angie, and they are in her bedroom, and he has climbed through her window, and they are both sixteen, and the sky outside is like the blown pupil of an eye, and the lateness of the hour is a covenant.

And sometimes when he sneaks through her window, they talk about the strangest things. And he remembers one conversation about bones, how she tells him she broke her wrist at age ten and how that wrist, when the cast came off, had grown accustomed to its stiffness and so refused to remember for a time the ways of motion.

And they talk about how weird it is that bones are invisible beneath the skin, how they jut close to the surface in places but don't show themselves otherwise…unless there is a terrible break or a person dies and the skin falls away.

And some nights in Angie's bed, they gaze out the window at the bones of the stars buried in the sky's mud, and Ethan remembers once seeing a homeless and shirtless man along the interstate, his ribs like the hulls of a ship, and Angie tells him how once her dad found the bones of mice inside their basement wall.

And Ethan says, I better get home before my dad notices.

And Angie says, You really think he would?

And Angie tells the story of how her grandmother died of a broken hip and how her aunt, when she moved to South Carolina, dug up the bones of her cat to take with her.

And when Ethan marries at the age of twenty-four and his father doesn't attend because he is in prison outside Detroit, the snow outside the apartment where he and Janice live looks, sometimes, like gray ash, like an occultation coming down. And Ethan, who wakes first most days, hears the soft tide of his wife's breaths as he climbs from bed. This is their life now. And one morning in the kitchen, he hears the otherworldly sounds of an owl from the woods behind the apartment complex. The creature seems to be saying something secretive to the falling snow. And Ethan, going outside and heading into those trees, remembers his father sometimes claiming that dead owls nailed to barn doors warded off evil spirits and that the call of an owl was a kind of numerology.

And he walks into those woods and plays a child's game: *If he finds the bird, he and his wife will be happy forever.* And he scans tree limbs that are barren with winter, that lift the gray skeletons of their arms. And behind him, his footprints are hieroglyphics in the snow, and he offers the wraiths of his breaths to the air. And he thinks—the memory appearing of its own volition—about his mother telling his father once that her chest from the surgery looked like a cut of beef in a butcher's shop. And Ethan hears a fluttering in a branch back in the direction from where he came, and he squints hard into the gray and sees some kind of blurred motion. Wings? And he wonders if his dad always had him say leukemia because it was another kind of cancer. And he walks inside the curtain of snow back to the house and has breakfast with Janice, and he wants to tell her something profound about his life, something that will draw the pieces of the fabric all together, but all he knows to say is, You sleep okay?

Through the Wall

LEWIS IS AWARE ON THIS COOL MARCH DAY OF THE DIFFERENCE between how things look and their secret inwardness. He thinks this while he and his wife—he loves the sound of "wife," how it feels both foreign and familiar—step from their apartment building and head toward the bus stop. Gail has a doctor's appointment. Their first child-to-be. Routine prenatal visit. The streets of Rogers Park on this latish afternoon are alive with commotion. Heads bob on the sidewalks. Pedestrians press by—schools of fish—or wait at street corners for the stoplights to work through their rotations. And everywhere the faces are the same. Blank. Noncommittal. The world made of automatons. Which is a lie, of course. The deceptive surface too often mistaken for everything. But the truth? Everyone they pass is consumed by some wondrous or desperate interior story. Tragedies and joys and fantasies and love and regret and anger and desire. Each person burning with some private furnace of being.

And Lewis's story? His with Gail? They are in love, of course. They are married now, not quite a year. Gail is five months along, due to give birth in July. Both she and Lewis will be free then, from teaching. Eugene Field Elementary. They will be able to devote themselves entirely to their daughter. The story inside them, in other words, is one of joy. But none of this can be seen, of course. In fact, all that is visible in this moment is how he and Gail grip hands as they hurry across the street and climb aboard the bus.

This does not mean, however, that marriage is turning out to be precisely what Lewis expected. It is, he is learning, a strange existence. He never imagined he might feel—and so profoundly—the mysterious migration of the days. He and Gail awaken in bed each morning, the Chicago traffic sounds seeping through their bedroom window, and they rise and listen to the splashing of water as they take turns showering. Or maybe they drink coffee in the tiny kitchen while passing pages of the *Tribune* back and forth, or they talk about work on their four-block walk to the school. Their first kiss, actually, was in Gail's deserted classroom, where they were surrounded at the end of the day by tiny desks and chairs. After school each day, they walk home together. This is their life. And what happens when they enter their apartment? They are alone in that enclosed space, there where their interior lives are somehow openly on display, shared with each other. Lewis and Gail talk within those walls and cook and maybe watch a movie. Lewis touches a hand to Gail's belly whenever the baby kicks. And so the three of them, in one sense, are one person now. That's how it feels, at least. They share this single life together.

Yet there is one peripheral fact of that existence, if Lewis is honest with himself, that he doesn't share, not with his wife. It's a small thing, in his view, but there it is. It concerns the young woman who lives in the apartment next to theirs, her door the one immediately before their own. Lewis sees the woman occasionally leaving or entering her apartment. And he hears her often through the walls: closing cupboards or watching television or flushing the toilet or speaking on the phone. And the woman is, to Lewis's way of thinking, very different from his wife, almost startlingly so. Gail, after all, is nearly six feet, with skin that freckles easily in summer and light-blond hair that bleaches in the sunlight. The neighbor woman, by contrast, is barely in her twenties—a full decade younger than either Gail or Lewis—and she is short and petite, with dark hair. And it seems unlikely she weighs more than a hundred pounds. And she is pretty, very. Almost doll-like in that prettiness, in contrast to Gail's athletic lankiness, her large bones. Lewis is aware of the attraction he feels for his neighbor, but it seems to him no more significant than what he might feel for an actress on a movie screen or a model in a television commercial. It's all surface, after all. It's like the light that shimmers on Lake Michigan in summer. No actual substance.

But the problem—and Lewis admits it is one—is that he can't stop thinking about her. There is something in her expression on the occasions when he spies her that he just can't shake. She appears, somehow, in the grip of some terrible sadness. Lewis is nearly certain of this. Or maybe she is simply weary. As though all her life is a burden. But why? Usually when he spies her in the hallway, she is dressed sharply, professionally, as though on her way to some high-powered job where she commands respect. Skirts and blazers, occasionally a pantsuit. Heels. Immaculate hair, drawn back with precision. A leather briefcase she carries as though it is filled with official and important papers. A lawyer? An up-and-comer in business? She can afford an apartment on her own, after all, while Lewis and his wife struggle with their two salaries combined, struggle even with some help from Gail's father. But whenever Lewis hears the sound of the neighbor's shower in the mornings, hears music existing ghostly in the walls, he imagines that there is something forlorn in her life, some hidden and profound sorrow. A lover who broke her heart? A deathly ill parent? An estrangement from her family? And he knows that he shouldn't feel this way, knows it is a bizarre fantasy to picture her in the throes of some discontent that probably—and he is aware of this as well—isn't real. But some nights when he is trying to sleep, he thinks of her sadness as though it is something you might hold in your hands. He imagines her lying in her bed beyond the wall, and he tells himself that sorrow can give any life its dignity, that this is something, somehow, to admire. And he pictures himself "saving her," as foolish and even offensive as he knows that sounds. Saving her from what? And he knows that the fantasy exists only on the borderline of consciousness. And each time he has these thoughts, he tells himself to come to his senses. Maybe he moves closer to his wife in bed, drapes an arm across her. Stupid fantasies don't diminish his love for Gail, after all. He curls against where she is curled, and their child is curled in her belly. What could this be if not love?

The woman's name, Lewis learns from the mailboxes in the lobby, is Miranda Watkins. He nods to her on occasion on the stairs, sees her one day carrying groceries in the hallway, notices her, on another, talking on her cell phone just outside the building. But the first time they speak more than a few polite words in passing is when Maggie is maybe four weeks old. Lewis and Gail are leaving their apartment with the baby just as their neighbor is entering the hallway in jogging shorts, T-shirt, athletic shoes. Maggie is in her stroller, and Lewis and

Gail are planning to take her on this humid Sunday afternoon on an excursion to Linden Park, hoping that the motion of the walk will encourage their young daughter to slip into sleep and give them some brief respite. Rarely, after all, does Maggie sleep in sustained spurts. Usually, it's no more than an hour or two at a time, punctuated, always, by fussiness. Lewis and Gail are exhausted, of course, though they tell each other that this is a good exhaustion, the exhaustion of love. And it is true that Lewis feels fiercely protective of his new child, as though he might fling himself willingly and without thought into the path of an oncoming bus should that somehow save her.

Now, the neighbor woman—*Miranda, Miranda,* he whispers sometimes in his thoughts—is bending down before their stroller. She makes soft sounds, cooing sounds. She says how perfect their little child is, how sweet she seems, how lucky they are as parents.

And suddenly the woman and Gail are talking on and on, laughing together. Gail says, "At the hospital one of the nurses told us what a sweet cry she has. We're not convinced. Not at all. I hope it doesn't bother you next door."

"No," the woman says. "Of course not. She's adorable." The woman stands as she says this, and she speaks her name to them. So of course they speak their names back. They all shake hands. They all smile. And Lewis sees the dark circles of perspiration beneath the armpits on Miranda's T-shirt. She has been out running, clearly. There is a faint salt scent about her, some distant sea. She is saying—apparently Gail has spoken again—that "Maggie" is a pretty name, a pretty name for a beautiful baby girl. All of them are smiling, as though someone has flipped a switch. But this is on the outside, of course. Lewis, as he gazes at the woman, is convinced that he sees lines and furrows of sadness around her eyes, sees the telltale slump of the shoulders, sees the way she seems reluctant, even, to draw in air. Is he imagining this? Is it possible, he suddenly wonders, that she lost a child of her own in the not-so-distant past? A miscarriage or even a young baby? Is that the source of her agony? The fact that she and Gail are throwing back their heads in unison as they laugh means nothing. This is only what exists in the world fabricated for others to see. A projection.

School resumes that fall. Maggie is in daycare across the street from Eugene Field. Lewis and Gail are back to their teaching lives, back to their classrooms. Gail remarks more than once that she hadn't realized how trying it would be to deal with a roomful of unruly children by day, then to pick up a crying Maggie at day's end. Lewis and his wife commiserate with each other. This becomes their ritual, their salve. They share the trials of being teachers, the trials of being parents. They say, too, how they wouldn't trade any of it for the world. These words remind Lewis, as they speak them, of the snow that soon will begin falling across Chicago as winter arrives. It will be city snow, of course. It will be silent coming down, mute, a beautiful and wordless dream, a perfect fantasy of white, and then—so quickly that it will seem its own small miracle—the snow will turn gray, become slush on the streets and even on the sidewalks, some glop of dark detritus. Lewis wants to explain all this to Gail, but he knows that there are words that are true and words that are some strange simulacrum of the truth. And how can he know for sure which is which? So he thinks, instead, and often, about the young woman who lives next door. *Miranda. Miranda.* It is a secret sound in his head, arriving like small, whispered waves. And he pictures himself knocking softly on her door. She admits him, of course. And her apartment is dark. Maybe candlelight flickers like some cuneiform writing on the walls. And she goes up on tiptoe as she wraps him in her arms. And she is real in this moment in his fantasy, fully corporeal. He can almost feel her body press against him, her lips press against his own. This is the kind of love that exists when Lewis sees Lake Michigan at night, the inky and moving waters alive with mystery.

It is early in January when it becomes clear there is a man. Lewis never sees him. Never sees him entering or leaving the apartment. But there is a voice now beyond the walls that does not belong to Miranda. Deep and rumbling. A masculine cough. Heavier footsteps. And does Lewis hear bed sounds? Maybe. He isn't sure. But he isn't jealous. Not really. There is something oddly thrilling in the thought of the sounds, something that takes him through the wall to be with Miranda. Can't he imagine, after all, that the voice is his? And isn't that enough? He has Gail and Maggie in his life, and he adores them both, but now he has this other life as well, his secret life, with Miranda. It is a complex and layered life, with so many surfaces he knows he might never arrive at the end. And it is true that he hears the man and Miranda arguing at times. Their angry voices like suds in the walls. Odd crashes. Volleys of fury. And then—by March—silence. Lewis keeps listening for that lower range of speech, but it is no longer there. It has vanished. It is just Miranda, just her voice on the phone, just her shower sounds. He sees her one evening out the living room window. Sees her on the street by the front entrance to the YMCA. She is walking rapidly along the line of cars pressing close to the curb, and he tells himself—back to that old story he cannot shake—that there is something tortured in the way she moves, the way she carries herself.

"Why do you act all the time like a caged animal?" Gail asks one night after they've put Maggie down to sleep, while she is sitting on the living room couch, watching television. Lewis is returning from the kitchen with a beer. Her words seem conjured out of nowhere, arriving of their own strange volition. Gail is in her penguin pajama bottoms. A Cubs sweatshirt. Her feet are bare. Her hair tied back. She turns to face him as he sits. This is in the middle of the show. Two characters are arguing over the best way to catch the murder suspect.

Lewis squints. "What are you talking about?" he says.

"Do you even want to live here?"

"What's going on?"

"Do you even want to be married to me? Be a father? Tell the truth, Lewis. For once in your life, tell the truth."

"Where is this coming from?"

"I see how you look. All the time. Okay? Don't think I don't see it."

"Look how? This is crazy. Of course I want to be with you. I love you. I love Maggie too. What's going on?"

"You know what I mean. I walk in a room and you look. . . well, disappointed."

"That's not true."

"It didn't used to be like that."

"It's not now. We're exhausted. Both of us. That's all. That's what you're seeing. It will get better when Maggie is a little older. You know that. You know I love you. You do."

Then she is in his arms. Her face is buried in his neck. His neck is damp from her tears. He holds her as she shakes with weeping. She feels real in this moment. The most real she has seemed in a long while. She wants to make love to him. Here. Now. On the couch. While the light from the television washes over them. They are kissing. They are getting undressed. They are happy. Aren't they? Isn't this a kind of happiness? The solid kind, the sort that lasts?

Yet Lewis worries. How could he not worry? What if he is a stranger now to his own interior life, and sees, somehow, only his own surfaces? It is such an unsettling idea. What if, in some secret recess to which he doesn't have access, he doesn't love Gail, doesn't want to be with her? What if, in some hidden version of himself, he regrets that he married her, regrets that he is a father, regrets that he has tethered himself to the constraints of this life. The thought pains him, sometimes, when he is reading to Maggie or holding her in his arms or singing to her. It pains him when he slips an arm around his wife or feels her body beside him in the bed at night, hears the tide of her breaths. And his fantasies are even worse. He creates such elaborate scenarios, long and involved stories. Interior novels of his life with Miranda. Maybe they have a secret tryst and fall in love, then run away to Hawaii or Alaska. Maybe Gail dies in some tragic accident, and Miranda becomes Maggie's mother. Grief, between them, becomes a kind of elixir. Or maybe the loud boyfriend returns and says rude things to Miranda, and Lewis tells the man in no uncertain terms that he has to leave...then comforts Miranda afterwards. Or maybe the building is on fire, and he carries Miranda, who has passed out from the smoke, down to the street. Lewis works through these fantasies until they seem like old friends, like those grooves in old-fashioned record albums set to life by a spinning turntable, a needle. Is it shameful to run through these fantasies while Gail is asleep beside him, while Maggie is asleep in the next room? They feel so real sometimes. Miranda, kneeling before him, gripping his knees, makes some grand confession. Some terrible secret she's been hiding all her life. He lifts her to her feet. *It's fine*, he says, *you'll be fine*. Then he wakes in the morning and rises. Wakes and talks to his wife over breakfast. Wakes and walks with her and Maggie out of the building to begin the day. And everywhere on the sidewalks and streets, everywhere Lewis looks, are blank faces of pedestrians, as blank as his own.

Soon it is summer again. The planet spins out on its rotations. The days blink their eyes and are gone. And then it happens. A weekday early morning. Lewis is heading down the stairs to go to the corner market. They are out of milk for Gail's coffee, Maggie's cereal. And just as he reaches the main doors of the apartment building, just as he is about to head down the three steps to the sidewalk, the sky opens and rain tumbles down. No preamble. Great sheaves of it. An onslaught of wet. Deafening in the lobby, as though there is nothing else in the world in this moment. Which is why, Lewis realizes, he doesn't hear Miranda coming up behind him in her heels, doesn't see her with her briefcase and her work skirt and her ironed blouse until she is standing almost directly beside him. She actually bumps him faintly as she attempts to peer outside.

"Shit," she says, then grins apologetically. She lifts her cell phone to check the time. "I'm late," she adds.

"It started out of nowhere," Lewis says. "Full bore."

"I guess I have to go back upstairs for my umbrella."

"It might be the sort that gives up quickly," Lewis says. "Then the sun comes back out. Schizophrenic storm."

"That's the technical term?"

Lewis nods, grinning. And Miranda grins too. And she is close enough that he notices a faint and pleasant odor. Coconutty? Shampoo? Perfume? Hand lotion? And her face is so near that her prettiness is somehow mesmerizing, dizzying. And they are talking as though they know each other, really know each other. They are, somehow, fast friends, and not just fellow travelers in a storm. He knows this is probably an illusion, but can't some illusions turn out, in the end, to be true? And then he does it. It shocks him. He doesn't know he is planning this until it happens. He reaches out with his left hand and places it lightly on her right elbow. He moves her slightly to the side. He does this because one of their fellow apartment dwellers—a very large middle-aged man who has an umbrella—is hurrying up behind them. The man presses past, nearly bumping Miranda. She does a little pirouette to avoid him. She offers Lewis a faint, thankful glance. *Thanks for getting me out of the way.* And it's hard to explain, but this is something shared. Some little moment between them. Miranda was nearly crushed by a huge and rude bowling ball of a man, and Lewis saved her. He recognizes the irony. Saved her. Like in his fantasies. And Miranda faintly rolls her eyes as though to joke, *I could have been killed. I could have been crushed.*

And Lewis realizes that he is still touching her elbow, even though the man is past them, even though the rain is even louder because the door is still open in that moment, even though the pummeling of the sidewalk and the street consumes everything. And in this moment, Lewis has a vision. A crazy vision. It startles him that this comes into his mind. He is going to bend down to kiss her. He is going to touch his lips to her lips. And what does he expect? That she will return the kiss, throw her arms around him, and draw him near? It is ridiculous. Utterly ridiculous. But isn't she gazing up at him? Staring directly into his eyes? Their eyes locking, as they say. And isn't there an intensity there, some emotional turmoil or churning? Is something happening? Actually happening?

She says, "I'm going to risk it."

For a single moment, he thinks she means kissing him. He thinks she is about to go up on her tiptoes in the exact manner she has done often in his fantasies. It is actually going to happen. In the real world, the outside world, the living world.

Then she is pushing through the door, and he understands. There has been a sudden faint pause in the rain, a held breath. And out she goes. Out into the world. He stumbles after her, but she is gone. A few huge fat drops still fall from the sky. Splatting around him. She hurries ahead on the sidewalk, holding her briefcase above her head. And he knows that whatever almost happened—if anything almost happened—it is gone forever. Never coming back.

And he is right. Exactly right. By August her apartment is occupied by an elderly couple with a small yapping dog. By August Miranda has vanished. Lewis doesn't realize this at first, though, until the morning Gail tells him. They are coming up the stairs—with Maggie—when they see the new neighbors leaving the apartment, their little dog on a leash, barking. *She moved in with her boyfriend*, Gail explains to Lewis when the couple is finally out of range. *I talked to her the day she was moving out. You didn't know? I wish we had her back. That dog's obnoxious.*

Lewis and Gail enter their apartment. They lift Maggie from her stroller and place her in her highchair. They are going to make lunch. Lewis begins cutting up fruit for the fruit salad. He starts with a cantaloupe. The seeds spill onto the cutting board, falling from the orange guts. He thinks about the first time he cut a cantaloupe as a child. His parents were gone from the house. Was he six, seven? He cut off a small flap of his left forefinger. The blood was red and insistent. He thinks about this as he slices. Gail, beside him, unwraps the store-bought pizza and places it on a metal tray, bumps him playfully with her hip. She smiles. He smiles back. He tries to read what she is thinking behind her eyes. He wonders what is living there, what life or lives. He wonders what thoughts gather then retreat. And his words spill out. "I love you," he says, just as Gail is opening the oven door to place the tray inside. A wall of warmth from the preheated oven presses toward Lewis, makes him back away. His words hang in the air, hang outside his body, hang there in the heat while his fingers are sticky with cantaloupe juice, and his face is flushed from the oven's heat. And Gail looks at him now, peering through half-closed eyes, squinting eyes. And what is she thinking? Her thoughts as blank to him now as anyone's on the street, as blank as someone Lewis might stand beside on an L train or in line at a pharmacy. Then Maggie, from her highchair, lets out such a sudden and piercing wail—for no reason that is apparent—that both Lewis and Gail turn. But their child seems fine, fine. . .

Gail turns to Lewis with an amused twist to her lips. She says while closing the oven door, "Such a sweet cry."

They roll their eyes in unison, and Lewis returns to slicing up the fruit.

Old Snow

THE HOUSE LOOKS OUT ON THE LAKE'S GLASS EYE. OLIVIA IS nine and her favorite game is imagining that the lake has secrets that only she and her brother understand. Often when she rises, she checks first thing out her bedroom window to see if the lake has gone missing in the night. But each time she leans against the windowsill, the lake is there. It is reliable. It sits past where her father's pickup is parked, the blue or green or gray waters waiting cross-legged, patient.

It is winter now. The yellowing cattails in the shallows are in sleepy decay. There is mealy snow—no longer young with sparkling teeth—on the ground beneath the gray Ohio sky. It is snow like a creature with its ribs showing. And the pickup is gone. In its place is something blank, something raw like a missing tooth.

Olivia moves down the hallway to the kitchen. Her brother's name is Troy. He is standing at the counter, sipping coffee. He is a junior in high school. He draws one of the chipped green bowls from the cupboard. He finds the Frosted Flakes in the nearly empty pantry. He lifts the milk from the fridge, sniffing it before placing it before her on the table. He performs all of this with a kind of playful rhythm, choreographed. Olivia applauds softly. Troy grins with a corner of his mouth. Half rolls his eyes. "Don't forget I work after school," he says.

"I know," Olivia says.

"Eat up, Silly," he says. "You need your sugar high."

"Yum, yum."

Troy's bus arrives before Olivia's, so she finds herself, as always, alone at the living room window. Waiting. The minutes are a held breath. They languish. The house breathes so quietly that it seems to be trying to sneak up on someone. Then finally she sees the smear of yellow turning onto the narrow road sidling close to the lake. She races from the house. Her breaths wave their little flags. She hears the whoosh as the doors come open. She climbs out of the cold, sits near the front with only her own company. She braces herself for a question she knows she cannot answer, though mercifully it never appears in the world.

Where's your dad?

Olivia's earliest memory is of being out on the lake in a rowboat. That's how she thinks of it: the lake. She knows it has another name, a longer one, but that longer one is reserved for strangers, for something to say on a map. What she remembers about the distant day is how far away it seems. She, her mother, her dad, and Troy were having a picnic in the boat. The oars weren't in the water but tucked around them like dripping wings. Olivia was eating a sandwich. Her eyes were narrow slits as she looked up at the bully of the sun.

Around her were the voices of her parents. They were a commotion. They crashed like bowling balls. Bumped against the clouds, slapped the glimmering surface of the water. Then suddenly her dad's hand twitched out. It was a familiar sight. A hand slept and slept and slept but then uncoiled.

The slap knocked Olivia's mother from the boat. The boat rocked like it wanted to be upside down. It was a horse kicking out with its back legs. Suddenly her mother was inside the wrinkled water. She was only her head, her shoulders. The lake swallowed the rest of her, possessed her. She was saying bad words. Troy reached out to try to help her back into the boat, but their mother was all kicks and long sweeps of her arms. Olivia watched her growing smaller and smaller as she swam away. Watched her when she stood finally in the shallows, the dark ink of her hair running down her back. Watched her climb out on shore and disappear into the trees.

Olivia thinks she remembers, too, her mother disappearing forever after that. In Olivia's mind, that was the same day her mother packed a suitcase and was gone. And so they have been looking for her ever since. Even inside the house, like a game of hide-and-seek. In dim closets. In the narrow envelopes under beds. In the cellar that is its own pretend lake after it rains. The way Olivia looks for her father now as well. Waiting to see him with his Pabst Blue Ribbon on the back porch. Waiting for his voice to once more be soapsuds in the walls.

Troy always tells her she has it wrong, though. He says, "It was the next summer she left. Don't you remember?"

"No," Olivia says.

"She sat us down. Promised to send for us. When she could. We'd live with her again. Without dad."

Always he speaks these words like he's reading from a picture book, one of the ones Olivia adored when she was younger. Like the words are etched there on the page. Are a bright drawing.

"Will we ever hear from her?" Olivia asks. Most evenings

the ritual is the same. Troy brings home food from Taco Bell. Because he works there after school and on weekends, he sometimes doesn't have to pay. Or he carries a small bag of groceries as he walks home. Often Gabby comes over, pushes through the back door without knocking. She has red hair and red-ant freckles. They crawl everywhere on her face. She and Troy kiss. They touch tongues, Olivia knows. She imagines that it's like spitting in someone's mouth. She suspects, too, what they do in Troy's room. Take off their clothes. Lie on each other like wrestlers trying to get the other one to hold still.

But for all that Olivia likes Gabby. Gabby helps her with her barrettes. Gabby wears perfume that makes a little wall of the air, something to step inside. The three of them watch TV on Gabby's laptop. Or Troy sits at the kitchen table and figures out which bills to pay. Or he tries calling their dad's cell one more time. Olivia hears the voicemail message in her head. It is stuck there, replaying itself like something she used to chant while jumping rope with her eyes closed.

"Maybe you should call the police," Gabby says.

"No," Troy says.

"I can tell my mom what's happened."

"No," Troy says.

"What if he never comes back?"

"He'll be back," Troy says.

"And that will make it better? Let me ask my mom. Maybe you can live with us."

"We're fine," Troy says.

"No, you're not," Gabby says.

Olivia is sent to bed earlier than she wants. She resents this. She has to be home by herself so long before and after school, and now she has to be alone in her room. She looks out her window at the lake. It is black beyond the lawn. It's a bruise. It is a sleeping bear. It is dreaming at the far end of the yard. If there's moonlight, the lake holds it with its arms, clutching it to the surface. If it's snowing, the lake sticks out its tongue to catch the flakes. Olivia climbs into bed, closes her eyes. Sleeping is like riding on a boat on a lake. She feels the waves rocking her, whispering. And what do they say? *I will be here when you wake up. I will be here.*

Gabby drives them. Her car is green on the outside. There is gray tape on a crack in the window beside where Olivia sits. From the backseat, she sees the world bounce up and down. It is a nervous world, fidgeting. Sometimes the snow becomes moths battering the windshield, or perching for a moment and holding on. In front, Troy is pointing. *Try this one. This one.*

These are the fancy houses. The houses that put on airs. On the opposite side of the lake from where Olivia and her brother live. Most of these houses are called *summer*, even though they exist year round. They hold their breaths in the winter, waiting. It's not the townies who live there, after all. No one lives there now. Gabby parks down the road from whatever house Troy picks. She and Troy sneak up along the shore of the lake. They pretend they are trees. They look for open windows, doors. If they do not find one, they look for a brick or a heavy stone. Olivia waits in the car. Her job is to call Troy on his cell if a police car slouches by on the road. If a neighbor stands on the winter grass and peers. Olivia waits alone in the car with her breaths, which swirl around her body like living spirits. She waits alone in the car with her fingers hiding in her mittens. Her nose is a little faucet. She waits.

Sometimes they return with treasure. A little cash to count between them in the front seat. A few coins. Once a watch that points to the minutes with a long skinny arm and the hours with a stub arm. Once a portable generator they pick up after dark along the river where they left it. Another time three fishing poles. Gabby and Troy sell the items on eBay. Another time it's a ring that Gabby slips on her own finger like she is proposing to herself. And still another time, Troy reaches a snow globe into the backseat. He turns it upside down and shakes it. He turns it back. Snow falls. Snow falls in the real world too. The two worlds are living suddenly in unison.

"Can I keep it?" Olivia asks.

"Sure thing," Troy says, winking.

Once their dad fell from the roof. Olivia remembers how he used a walking stick to pound on the floor of his room. The floorboards shook, cried out. The pounding said they should bring something to him or they were making too much noise. It was winter but their father couldn't work the snowplow. It was winter but they had no money. In the summers, when there was construction work, their father sometimes splurged and bought them clothes or new phones. One night, while still recovering from the fall, their dad beat Troy with that same walking stick. Afterward, Troy sat in the backyard in the snow. Olivia went out to sit beside him. The moon sat with them as well, saying nothing. It was so cold that Olivia's behind went numb. When finally she went back in, she touched her behind but it wasn't there. Somehow it had vanished. She could see her finger push against it, but nothing existed.

Olivia thinks about this memory the same night Troy begins

talking to Gabby about St. Paul.

"I think that's where our uncle lives," he says.

"You'll go live with him?" Gabby says.

"I doubt it," Troy says. "He and my dad never talk. I don't think I've ever met him."

"Where's your mom's family from?"

"Florida, maybe," Troy says. "I'm not really sure."

"You can't get away with this forever," Gabby says.

"I know," Troy says.

Olivia asks Gabby, "Are freckles catching?"

"What?" Gabby asks. Her head is on Troy's shoulder. Only one eye is visible to Olivia. That eye squints.

"Like poison ivy," Olivia says.

"What are you talking about, Ovie?" Troy says. It's a version of how she used to say her name when she was little.

"Did the freckles start on her face then spread?"

There is a musty pillow on the couch. It smells like someone's wet dog. Troy begins playfully hitting her with it. It smells like dog breath. Pummeling her.

"Is silliness catching?" Troy asks. Then suddenly he sits up straight, makes a formal stiffness of his shoulders.

"Don't say it," Olivia says.

He clasps his lips together, at the ready.

"Don't," Olivia says.

"Bedtime," Troy says.

Olivia collapses on the couch like she's been shot. She lolls back her head, lets her tongue stick out. Air moans from her throat like from a deflating balloon.

"Now," Troy says.

It is summer. School is out. Bullfrogs have something loud to say to the night air. Fireflies wink light into the backyard. Troy works long hours at Taco Bell, but when he's home there are often strangers knocking on the door, ringing the doorbell. Often there is a smell in the house like someone dug up the rich loam of a garden. It smells like smoke made of mud. Troy and Gabby smoke sometimes in the house, but mostly they hand over sandwich bags to whoever arrives at the door. In exchange for cash. Troy and Gabby and Olivia are rich now. Troy buys a new Xbox. He buys Olivia new flipflops. They are tight between her toes, gripping her with what she imagines is love.

One night Troy and Gabby let her take a few puffs. "Not too much," Troy says. The world goes loose on its axis. Colors smudge. Blur. Olivia feels like her tongue is alive in her mouth. It is a small amphibian. It does what it wants. She touches it with a finger and it twitches. She dances with Troy in the living room. She kicks off her flipflops and stands on his feet. She says suddenly with that frog tongue, "He's coming home soon. I know it."

The music throbs in the room. It takes up space. It claims the air. Troy says over it, "Dad? You mean Dad?"

"Yes," she says.

"I don't know," Troy says. "He might have pulled a mom."

"Never," Olivia says.

She pictures her dad stepping through the front door. He told them before he left he had a construction job in Pennsylvania, would be back in three weeks. He sat them down in the kitchen, plopped his hands on his knees. Olivia watched those hands in case they twitched. He told them that when he got back he'd have cash. He told them not to tell anyone he was gone. Their little secret. Like something that would fit in a pocket.

"I'll be back," he'd said as he stepped out the door. The voice existed in a movie, Troy explained. Their dad was talking from inside a movie.

"He'll be back," Olivia says now, but she doesn't know if the voice is right. Her voice sounds like it has smoke-loam inside it. Like it is floating.

Gabby is an absence. One night over supper Olivia realizes that she just isn't there. Hasn't been there for several days. Has blinked off like a firefly.

"Where's Gab?" Olivia says.

"Eat your pizza," Troy says.

"But where's Gab?"

"Things happen," Troy says.

"She left us?" Olivia asks.

"Eat your pizza," Troy says.

The next day is Sunday. Troy takes her swimming. The lake distorts their legs as they wade in. Makes them seem fat, like stub legs. They lie on their backs on floats. Olivia's float is yellow. She closes her eyes and sees the pink behind her eyelids. She closes her eyes and feels heat like a lotion on her skin, an actual weight. The tiny waves make her bob like someone is under her and gently pushing at the float. A motorboat goes by. A teenage girl is water skiing in a bikini. The wake makes Olivia's float bounce up and down like it is angry. The lake is a small whip. Someone cracked it.

When they wade back to shore with their floats, Gabby is standing in their backyard. Tears stain her cheeks. She rubs the back of her hand beneath her nose. She is in bare feet, her sandals kicked off. She runs across the grass with her tears and hugs Troy. Her arms loop their way around his neck to make a close circle. Then Gabby asks to hug Olivia too.

"Come here, Ovie," she says.

A tear falls on Olivia's head. She feels it drop there. It trickles down her scalp, a baby river.

It is snowing in the summer. Olivia is outside playing with her snow globe. She turns it over and watches glitter fall. She is sitting in the front yard when Mrs. Pitford walks over from across the road. Mrs. Pitford has hair the same color as the falling snow. Her hair is a snowflake.

Mrs. Pitford says, "Is your father home?"

Olivia blinks. Blinks. Maybe when she opens her eyes, Mrs. Pitford will be gone.

"I haven't seen his truck for a long time," Mrs. Pitford says.

Olivia blinks. Blinks. "It broke," she says. The words arrive of their own volition, conjured by her tongue.

"Is he home now?" Mrs. Pitford asks.

"No," Olivia says. She is clutching her snow globe to her chest. Her snow globe will protect her. She is standing. She is starting toward the house.

"Can you tell him I'd like to talk to him?" Mrs. Pitford asks.

Olivia doesn't answer. The words bounce off her back. She hurries inside and closes the screen door. She peers out the living room window. Mrs. Pitford is walking back to her house. She pats a hand to the top of her snowflake hair. Like she's telling that hair, *Good job.*

"We'll adopt you when we're eighteen," Troy says one evening when all of them are on floats, Gabby too. Gabby's float is also yellow. Their floats match.

"We'll get married and adopt you," Gabby says.

"We'll go live somewhere else," Troy says. "Maybe Florida. Do you want to live in Florida, Ovie?"

"I want to live on a cloud," Olivia says. "Can we live on that cloud there?" She points. The cloud holds still, like it is holding its breath.

"I don't know about that," Troy says.

"I'll be your mom," Gabby says. She giggles. Her float shakes, like it's giggling too.

"Why do you want to live on a cloud?" Troy asks.

"Not any cloud," Olivia says. "That cloud."

"Why that one?" Gabby asks.

"It's over the lake. We can look down at our house."

"I hate to break it to you, Ovie," Troy says, "but clouds move."

"Not this cloud," Olivia says. "This one you can drive like a car. We'll drive it round and round over the lake."

"Okay," Troy says.

"Okay," Gabby says.

"Okay," Olivia says.

Fireworks over the lake aren't on the Fourth but the day before. People crowd the shore. Lie on blankets. Gabby, Troy, and Olivia watch from the backyard. The sky is made of flowers. Flowers that bloom then disappear, bloom then disappear. Each one makes a crack in the sky. Each flower makes the ground tremble. The sky flowers are every bright color. The sky flowers make Olivia clap her hands. The sky flowers make Troy and Gabby kiss. It's a perfect night. Both Olivia's brother and Gabby tuck Olivia into bed. This is her life now. She closes her eyes and pictures the flowers still blooming there, blooming back behind her eyes, behind the lake of her eyes.

In the morning she wakes and climbs from bed. Crosses to the window. Looks out. The lake is still there. It is winking at her. Then she notices something else. Something that makes her breaths grow still inside her chest. Her chest can't move. Her chest constricts. Her chest grips her tightly, holding on.

Her dad's pickup is back in its spot.

In the kitchen her dad is arguing with Troy. Troy is leaning with his back against the refrigerator. His face is flushed with anger, like someone took a pale red crayon to his cheeks, and carefully filled them in. Olivia's dad is leaning back in his chair, his hands behind his head, holding his head in place. His graying hair is clipped as close to his skull as grass on a putting green. His beard is missing, like it snuck away.

"Hey, Olive Oyl," he says, gesturing for her. Then he has her in his arms, enfolding her with cigarette smell, beer smell, dad smell. Then she is sitting in his lap, there in the saddle of her dad.

"Olive Oyl," he says again. It's a cartoon. Olivia knows he is calling her a cartoon name. His voice is a bulb turned low. Soft. It sounds like an apology.

"Dad," Olivia says. The word parts her lips and exposes her teeth. The word is spindly in the air, unsure of its positioning.

"Did you miss your old man, Sweet Pea?" he says.

"Fuck you," Troy says.

Olivia pretends she has turned to stone. Is motionless on her father's lap. If she doesn't breathe then maybe she is safe.

"What did you say?" her dad says.

"You heard me," Troy says, his voice riding up and down an invisible seesaw.

"What did you say to me?" her dad says again.

"I said you just left us here. All this time. Without a word."

"I explained that."

"It's not good enough," Troy says. "It's not fucking good enough."

"Are you going to cry now?" Olivia's dad says. "Is that what's going to happen? Over how hard things are? How tough your life is? Give me a break."

"Fuck you, Dad."

The big hands grip Olivia's arms and lift her off his lap. The big hands press into her flesh. Then her dad is up to his full height. There in the syrup of morning light pouring into the kitchen. His arms loose at his sides.

Troy is running now. Out the back screen door. The door slaps loudly, banging. A sound like a loose hinge. Olivia sees Troy through the screen mesh. Running with bare feet across the grass. Down toward the blue iris of the lake. He runs along the shoreline, away. And Olivia hears the loud breaths of her dad in the kitchen, the breaths rising from the dark caves of his lungs.

"Your brother sure is a drama queen," he says, winking. "I forgot what a drama queen he is. I'm going to get some shut eye now, Olive Oyl. I'm exhausted. If Troy-Boy slinks back, tell him we'll have some words later. I've got some words all picked out. Okay? Okay? It really is good to see you, Sweat Pea. I've missed you." His lips scrape her forehead. "You're a great kid, but I've really got to sleep."

The summer is hazy after that. It is like heat rising from the ground and making ghost waves that levitate in air. Troy's voice is always loud inside the house. Their father's voice is always loud inside the house. Olivia learns only slowly what happened. Their dad was arrested. Their dad spent time in jail. It was something about a fight in a parking lot. Someone had his face broken. In Pennsylvania. But their dad didn't tell anyone there were kids by themselves back in Ohio. He said to Olivia and Troy that he left that part out. *For your own good*, he said. *So you wouldn't be put in foster care. Did you want to be put in foster care?* Voices argue about this inside the house while Olivia is trying to sleep, make loud drumbeats in the house, thud voices. Olivia imagines that a cloud above the lake is her refuge. She imagines floating on that cloud above the house, floating far away from the voices. Mostly the voices say, *I hate you, hate you*. They say, *I wish you never came back*. They say, *You have a mouth on you*. They say, *Yeah, you better not let me catch you*.

By the next summer Troy is gone. With Gabby. Three days after Troy's eighteenth birthday. They pack up Gabby's green car. They hug Olivia as though they are trying to squeeze her insides out. She watches the car raise dust on the road, little veils that lift their tired selves into the air then fall back down. To Colorado, they are heading. Olivia rolls that name on her tongue, feels the twists of it, the convolutions.

Then Olivia walks down to look at the lake. The lake looks back. They stare at each other in silence. The lake is a held breath. The lake is a shimmering cloth. The lake is forever. Cattails dance faintly in the wind. Sway with their eyes closed.

Water sloshes close to her feet. Water whispers but not in words.

Olivia has her snow globe in her hands. She turns it over. Shakes it. Turns it back. Her father is standing on the back porch. She turns to show him, but he is too far away. She walks up to stand beside him. She shakes the globe then lifts it before him. It is snowing in the world inside her hand. The world there is snowing.

Dancing in Their Dead Mother's Dresses

LISTEN. THE THUMP OF THE MUSIC IS THREADBARE ON THIS Sunday afternoon. It is a faint pulse, and somehow needful. It makes of the living room in this small Escanaba home a mesmerizing dirge. How else is there to explain the sisters twirling with their eyes closed, the sails of fabric billowing as they turn? Both girls are in bare feet. The carpeting is so worn beneath them that it is possible to hear the sorrow of the floorboards. And the August sunlight—dropping past the curtains, dropping past the worn couch and across the scuffed coffee table—appears somehow broken. The girls dance sometimes into the bright tea of light, then dance away. The light doesn't notice, doesn't care. The girls aren't dancing with each other. They are dancing with the dresses that are far too long on them, trippingly long. One dress is floral. Ruth, eight, is wearing that one. The other is a pale yellow eye. That's Allison, age nine. Both girls have long and thin brown hair—as straight as though ironed—that swirls its little veil around them. Both girls have skinny arms and legs with chigger bites. The dresses belong to their mother. *Belonged* to their mother. And still the music plays. It lifts from one of those old-fashioned phonographs that rotates on its forever wheel. The needle scratches sometimes, skips to a new thought. The phonograph is in the corner of the room by curtains so heavy they somehow droop. And the music? It is the mother's music, grown up music. What she used to play when she danced with her girls. For this, after all, is Julia's game her girls are playing. What she taught her children. To pick a dress from her closet then to traipse. To imagine that their bodies were flowers bending in the breeze of the music, that their bodies were loose-fitting and so becoming something else.

And still the girls dance. From time to time they spin too close and lightly collide then bounce away. Four eyes come open when this happens.

"Watch it!" Allison says angrily.

"You watch it," Ruth says, though her tone is defensive, less sure of itself.

And this is the life of the girls, dancing while their father—does he even hear them? does he register that they have changed into his wife's garments and are playing her music in the next room?—smokes in the kitchen while looking out the window. Earlier that afternoon, after church—the family is Methodist—the father drove his daughters to the cemetery so they could place fresh flowers by the grave. Though mainly what happened was that Ruth grew distracted by a chattering squirrel high in a tree not far from the grave. The squirrel seemed to be complaining, was in a rile, and Ruth kept leaning her head back and back to see the creature, until she nearly lost her balance. And the squirrel, with the sun behind it in the green tree, was a blur of light, and dizzying. Ruth focused her entire life's attention on the squirrel, until Allison, annoyed, jabbed her roughly in the arm with an elbow… and Ruth remembered to clasp her hands soberly before her, and pray.

And Allison herself? She kept trying to picture the story her father had told her and her sister about their mother. About how she came to lie there in the ground instead of in her bed at night. Allison wanted to unravel the words. They were wound in knots. They were stubborn in her head. Their father, the story went, had picked up her mother in the car. Picked her up at Grandma's house on the far western side of town. And then they were on their way home. In the rain. Allison pictured the rain running its hand across the road, running its hand across the windshield. It was spiteful rain. Then the car slid off the road and went into a gully near the viaduct on Peterson Avenue. That's what Allison's father said. And somehow they struck the concrete of that viaduct. In the story it sounded as though this were almost a magic trick. One moment everything was fine in the rain, and in the next moment the future lives of the family had changed forever. Poof. That's, at least, how it sounded in the story. And what, Allison kept thinking, had happened to her father? He had a bruise that had turned his right elbow into a bright plum. He had a broken left wrist wrapped in a hard cast. He had a chipped front tooth when he pulled his lip away. That was it. And in the cemetery, after church, Allison's father was still wearing that white cast, still wearing the elbow bruise (though it was yellow now, and not visible beneath his dress shirt), wearing his chipped tooth. The cast covering his wrist was no longer such a perfect white. It was old snow. Allison kept staring at it. It made her furious to see it. Her father told them again to pray, but all Allison could think to say to God in her head was, *Why did you do this to me?*

Later, on the car ride back to the house, she sat glumly in the front seat and glared at her father as he drove. The car was not their old car. That one was gone. It, too, was poof. This was the new one their father had bought that very week. Though it was old. And sickly green. With a smelly inside. The car made rattling sounds like it didn't want to be traveling on the road, like it wanted to rest somewhere forever. And as Allison stared at her father, she kept trying to make him seem real to her eyes. For that was the thing. Since her mother had died, her father had seemed a ghost. This made no sense. Wasn't it her mother who ought to be the ghost? But it was her mother who was always present now, always there in each breath, each thought, each moment. If, in life, her mother had existed only when she was there in the room, now that didn't seem to matter. Her mother might have been Allison's own shadow, might have been the breaths she blew from her lungs into the air. Her mother filled everything now, overwhelmed everything. Her father seemed tiny beside that. He looked smaller than he used to. He drove with his shoulders slumped. He drove with his hair sticking up on his head like the short bristles on a brush. He said almost nothing. His words had fled him and wouldn't come back. It was like he had climbed inside himself and had closed the door. And his voice was so soft in those rare moments when he spoke that it almost couldn't be heard. Didn't he used to be louder? Didn't he used to exist more? And Ruthie was no better. It annoyed Allison sometimes. How her dumb little sister seemed to understand so little about what was going on, about how their lives had been destroyed, about how everything that had ever mattered was gone. *Wake up*, she wanted to yell at her sister. *Pay attention!*

And what stupid thing did Ruthie do in the car on the ride away from the cemetery? Ruthie was sitting in back while Allison was in the passenger seat, the same seat where, in the other car, her mother had died. Allison looked over the top of the seat and saw how, in back, Ruthie had her little hands clasped together. Not tightly. Like something was hiding inside there. Waiting. And every now and then Ruthie lifted her hands toward her face and opened them like a secret. Peered in.

"What's that?" Allison said, turning completely in the seat, aiming the disapproval of her eyes across the space between them.

Ruth looked up. Looked into the annoyance that was her sister now. And all Ruth could think was *she can't know, can't*. So Ruth put her hands in her lap and pretended to look out the window at the passing green. It was a blur green. There were houses, too. And the blur blue of the bay. Ruth knew her sister was mad at her now, mad because—according to Allison—she didn't appreciate what had happened. Allison made it sound like she couldn't remember it, like her mother was a pair of socks Ruth had borrowed and couldn't remember where she'd left them. But that was wrong. Ruth knew what had happened to her mother. She did. Death was the main thing now about her. Her gone mother. How could she not know that? At church just that morning, Allison had heard a boy in the pew in front of them say *Mom*. It was a jolt to hear the word floating so suddenly in the air, perching. Like the time she touched the toaster and got a shock. Right there in her body, shooting up through her fingers. So Ruth knew. She did. But that was separate from the fact that Allison couldn't know what she held inside her hands. Allison would be mad. She would. Ruth didn't know why—this was always the mystery now—but she was certain it was true. Allison would make that face. Like Ruth had insulted their mother. Like Ruth had made her even more dead.

"Open your hands," Allison said.

"No," Ruth said.

So the moment Ruth heard the gravel drive beneath the car, the moment the car was stopping before their house, the moment they were all climbing out into the midday sun, Ruth made a tight seal with her cupped hands. The sunlight squinted at her. The sun was a weight. She walked into it.

It took Allison two seconds to pry open her fingers.

"Why do you have *that*?" she said.

Ruth said nothing.

"Why?" Allison repeated.

Ruth still said nothing.

"You got it at the cemetery? What's wrong with you?"

"It's a grasshopper," Ruth said.

"Are you stupid? It's dead."

Allison slapped Ruth's hand. The brownish-greenish insect fell. Its wings didn't flutter. Just dropped. To the grass. The insect was tilted on its side. A tiny handkerchief.

Ruth lunged. She almost had it, but then Allison was pushing her toward the house, pushing hard. Ruth waited for her father to speak. *Stop it*, he would say, *stop*. Instead he kept walking up the sidewalk. Toward the front door. So there was just the sun with its bright eye. Just the heat of day. Just the way the heat was a hand pressing down.

And she kept thinking about the sun and the grasshopper while they sat—the three of them—at the kitchen table. Their father made them bologna sandwiches. The mustard smeared on Ruth's fingers. The mustard was sun colored. She licked the sun from her fingers. The real sun, the actual sun, fell through the windows while she licked. And she thought about what her sister was saying to her mother. The complaining tone. How much she hated Escanaba. She kept repeating it over and over. Escanaba, Escanaba, Escanaba. As though it were to blame. As though the sound of it had caused everything. Escanaba. And their father was smoking now. There was one large bite out of his sandwich, and then there was the smoke with its gray-blue curl. Ruth stared at the sandwich bite. It was the shape of teeth. It was something torn away. She stared at the orange flare as her father inhaled. Some little birth of light. Some flame of shriveling. And she saw her sister with her sandwich in both hands. And she thought of the grasshopper in the grass. Near where their mother would sometimes place the sprinkler for them. The sprinkler would arch its back. Tilting. They would run, run. The water was usually giggling cool. Ruth's bathing suit was blue. The grass would be slick, slippery. Now her mother was dead. Allison was wrong: Ruth knew it. She wondered if the grasshopper had known it was dying. If it had lain down in the cemetery grass and thought: *this is where I'm supposed to be*. Maybe Ruth should have left it there. Left it near the stone wall. She remembered a goldfish once floating at the top of the tank at her best friend's house. Margie. They were inseparable at school. But when Ruth touched the squirmy wetness, the fish wiggled and swam down, down, frantic. Should she touch the grasshopper? Should she sneak out the front door? Carry it up to the room she shared with her sister? Hide it beneath her pillow? Lie awake at night and think: *Allison doesn't know. She doesn't.*

"Put your dishes in the sink," their father said suddenly. His words passed through the smoke, came out the other side.

So Ruth hurried to leave her plate and glass in the bowl of the sink, hurried into the living room. She tried to sneak out the front door. She was going to place the grasshopper inside the top of one of her socks, place it where Allison would never see it. The grasshopper would hide there, ducking down. Where no one would know. And Ruth was going to carry it up to her bedroom and hide the insect inside one of her dresser drawers, or inside her pillowcase. After all, Allison couldn't tell her what to do. Allison couldn't tell her she couldn't have it. She had her hand on the knob to the front door. She felt it turning, turning.

"Where are you going?" Allison said. She had just stepped from the kitchen.

Ruth tried to hurry out. The big door was open. Now she had to open the screen door. She could see the sunlight like a smear on the front stoop and then the lawn, turning half of the lawn much brighter than the other, a fire. She would see where the grasshopper surely waited in the green, beckoning.

"You're not going out there," Allison said.

"Let go," Ruth said, for her sister now had hold of her arm. Her sister was tugging, dragging. Her sister was strong. It was one thing Ruth hated about Allison sometimes. How easily she dragged Ruth back into the living room. Ruth tried to grab hold of the doorknob to the big door, but it was no use.

Then they were both wrestling. Ruth felt the sway and pressure of their bodies, their pushiness. Then, somehow, they were on the floor. On the carpet. It smelled like feet. And Allison was on top of her, sitting on top of her, her weight like sinking deep to the bottom of a murky pond. There was no getting loose. *Are you stupid?* her sister was repeating. *Why are you stupid?*

Then Allison had her hands around Ruth's neck. Ruth could feel the fingers jabbing in. The vice of them. They were probing fingers, intrusive. And Ruth couldn't breathe. She couldn't breathe in her chest where Allison was sitting. She couldn't breathe in her neck where Allison was choking. And the thought occurred to Ruth that she was going to be dead. Like her mother. It served Allison right. It's what Allison deserved. To be alone. To lose first her mother, now her sister. Ruth hated her sister in this moment, wanted the worst for her.

But suddenly Allison rolled off. Ruth gasped. She was that goldfish with its open mouth near the top of the tank. The sisters lay on their backs. Lay side by side. Staring together at the ceiling. There were cracks in it, little lines like lightning bolts. It was like something lived there. Like something might suddenly peek out.

Ruth said to her sister without thinking, "What do you want to do?" Wasn't that what one or the other always said?

Allison said nothing.

Ruth lifted her hands above her body. Turned her palms toward her so she could see them. Where the grasshopper had been.

And suddenly her sister said, "Let's put on Mom's dresses."

So they did. They did. They climbed the creak of stairs. They stood in the dim of the closet. With its clothes smells. The wood smells. The dust smells. They rustled their hands and bodies through the dresses. Swirled through the dresses. The fabric made whispering sounds, secret sounds. They stripped out of their church clothes. Left them in a heap. Stripped down to their underthings. Then slipped into the dresses. Glided into them. Then headed back down the stairs. Put on the music. Allison did this since their mother wasn't there. Then they were dancing. *Are* dancing. As simple as that. Listen: the thump of the music is threadbare. It is a faint pulse. It is needful. And the girls are twirling across the living room, and then their father—he can't be forgotten altogether—emerges from the kitchen to lean against the wall, smoking. He rests his shoulder against the wallpaper with its small, red flowers. He watches as his girls dance. And what is he thinking? There must be a weariness inside his thoughts, if weariness counts as a thought. For the words in his head droop and slump. Are too tired to lift themselves. Too numbed. Like fingers first aching in winter cold then soon forgetting they are there. The girls, meanwhile, see the smoke rising from their father's cigarette. They put on a little show for that smoke. They twirl a little harder. Spinning out and out. They are the planet now, rotating on some axis no one sees. And the girls close their eyes and feel the music inside their bodies, inside the fabric of the dresses, inside their thoughts. And the music has no place else to go or be, no other way to pass the time. It is devoted to this moment and no other. And the girls dance into that music. They dance, for a time, holding each other's hands, but then they break away again. They dance until there are stitches in their sides, until they can hardly breathe, until their legs ache. But still they dance, their bare feet thumping the floor, their arms waving an imaginary language. Some choreography of signs. And sometimes they lift the folds of the dresses and dance them up and down, dance them as though they might suddenly come alive.

About the Author

DOUG RAMSPECK IS THE AUTHOR OF TEN COLLECTIONS OF poetry, two collections of short stories, and a novella. His latest books include *Smoke Memories* (winner of the Lena Shull Book Award, Redhawk Publications, 2025), *Blur* (winner of the Tenth Gate Prize, The Word Works, 2023), *Book of Years* (Cloudbank Books, 2021), *Under Black Leaves* (winner of the novella prize, Etchings Press, University of Indianapolis, 2020), *Distant Fires* (winner of the Grayson Books Poetry Prize, 2020), and *Black Flowers* (LSU Press, 2018). Other books are *The Owl That Carries Us Away* (2018), winner of the 2016 G. S. Sharat Chandra Prize for Short Fiction, and *Original Bodies* (2016), winner of the Michael Waters Poetry Prize and published by Southern Indiana Review Press. He is also the author of *Mechanical Fireflies* (2011), selected by Mary Ruefle for the Barrow Street Press Poetry Book Prize, *Possum Nocturne* (2010), and *Black Tupelo Country* (2008), which received the 2007 John Ciardi Prize for Poetry. His chapbook, *Where We Come From*, appeared in 2009.

Hundreds of Ramspeck's poems have been published by literary journals that include *The Kenyon Review*, *Slate*, *The Georgia Review*, *TriQuarterly*, *The Southern Review*, *The Sun*, and *The*

Missouri Review. His short fiction has appeared in *Southwest Review*, *Iowa Review*, *Narrative*, *The Southern Review*, *The Georgia Review*, *South Carolina Review*, *Cincinnati Review*, and many others.

He is a three-time recipient of an Ohio Arts Council Individual Excellence Award, a finalist for the UNT Rilke Prize, and the winner of the McGinnis-Ritchie Award for Fiction.

His short story, "Balloon," was listed as a Distinguished Story of 2018 by *The Best American Short Stories*.

His flash fiction story, "Snow Crow," received First Place in the Bath Flash Fiction 19th Award.

Married to Beth Sutton-Ramspeck—a Victorianist and Harry Potter scholar—Ramspeck is a retired Professor of English from The Ohio State University and lives in Black Mountain, North Carolina.

IU South Bend Publishing Center

The College of Arts & Science's Publishing Center at Indiana University South Bend, known as the Pub Hub, was established in 2017 with a mission to provide students with professional experience in the publication and production of works in print and digital media. IU South Bend students were involved in this project at every stage of development, from the initial manuscript to the final printed book. Kelcey Ervick is the director of the Pub Hub. We are proud to partner with Wolfson Press on this publication.

Associate Editor
Jessie Jimenez received her Master of Arts in English from IU South Bend in 2026. She worked at the Pub Hub from 2023–2026 and was the lead student editor throughout the book's production.

Assistant Editor
Theodore Ervin is pursuing a Bachelor of Arts in English with minors in Creative Writing and Publishing. He joined the Pub Hub in 2025.

Editorial Assistants
Michelle Hover, Keri Garrett, Jaiden Miller

Designers
Mali Bonnell, Julia Moreno